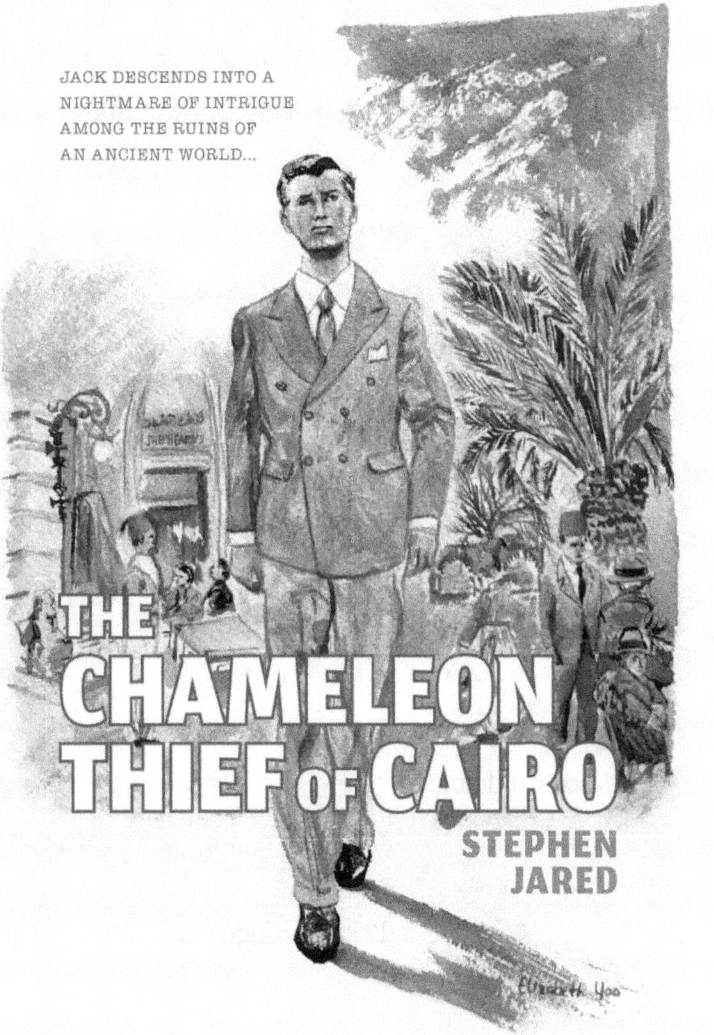
JACK DESCENDS INTO A
NIGHTMARE OF INTRIGUE
AMONG THE RUINS OF
AN ANCIENT WORLD...
THE
CHAMELEON
THIEF OF CAIRO
STEPHEN
JARED
Elizabeth Yoo

ALL RIGHTS RESERVED

Cover Art:

Cover art by Elizabeth Yoo

Design by Gilles Verschuere

Publisher's Note:

Solstice Publishing - www.solsticepublishing.com

The Chameleon Thief of Cairo

Stephen Jared

INTRODUCTION

In previously published stories, I referred to the challenge of chronicling the life of Jack Hunter. I hope you'll allow me to indulge on the difficulty of the task.

Over time, story details can play musical chairs. Reality tends to get pushed around by fantasy. I learned this as a boy when, on occasion, I'd ask Jack to recite a story he already told. So many moments in his life held me in suspense, or made me laugh out loud, and I wanted to hear them again. Hearing them again revealed changes and embellishments in the stories. Undoubtedly, some of this arose because of his past in Hollywood. He was a great storyteller. I suspect age also became a factor.

Although he never developed serious memory problems, every once in a while, Jack could succumb—and this may come as a surprise—to a dark mood. I only ever witnessed this after the passing of Max, the great love of his life. Even I can forget that, though his stories were larger than life, and at times difficult to believe, he was irrefutably human, prone to fears and frailties. On such days, a villain from his past who was previously hilarious, could turn terrifying. Accordingly, the absolute true version of all his stories remains somewhat elusive.

I've done my best to tell this story as it really happened. I recognize there are elements here with which society continues to struggle. Nonetheless, you'll have to forgive my shortcomings in that I'm incapable of casting a wide enough net around this little piece of history in order to make some grand statement on international affairs.

As a child, I simply found the story amusing. I enjoy spy stories, and vividly recall my shock when Jack told me he once was involved in a cloak-and-dagger adventure. When I look back on it today, it seems to retain a fair amount of charm.

CHAPTER ONE

Dark thunderclouds still carried flashes of lightning after three days of rain. New were a handful of distant white billowy forms, visibly shifting. Some light penetrated the violence of the heavens, and as the year was 1948 one couldn't help but frequently reflect on the unfathomable price paid during the war. Looking out from his bathroom window, Jack Hunter had a towel around his waist and shaving soap over his whiskers.

After large-scale horror, few things meant so much as friendly nods from strangers, handshakes at ball games, pie and ice cream with neighbors, simple things. Embrace the simple things, Jack repeatedly told himself. Trust the world had learned a thing or two. It wasn't easy. He looked out at his soaked Texas land, horses under shelter, and a flutter of birds unbearably small against clashing skies, and he too felt very small.

Before returning to his mirror, something caught his eye. An automobile sat stalled beneath a mesquite tree. He squinted, looking for movement as roiling clouds let out a rumble. Jack's wife, also visible from the second floor bathroom window, marched through storm colored puddles heading for what looked like a DeSoto. Jack wiped the shaving soap from his face with his towel, and quickly slipped into a pair of slacks. A moment later, he was out the front door and splashing across grass trying to catch up to the woman who remained the great love of his life.

By the time Jack reached the DeSoto, Max had the driver's side door open. Inside sat an elderly man thrown from the road by the overnight wind and rain. Blood oozed from a gash on his head; thin lips struggled for words. Had he been out here all night? Jack wondered.

He wore an elegant and finely tailored suit, and after Max checked the breast pocket, she said, "Ever hear of Marshall Kitchener?"

Before Jack could respond, the man raised a trembling hand, and pinched the bridge of his nose. He tapped slim fingers to his gash, and his eyes flickered. "I'll be fine," he said, with a voice sounding as though it had been raked through a desert. "I'll be fine," he repeated.

"Listen, mister," Max said, "You smacked into this beautiful tree of ours pretty good. I don't think this DeSoto's taking you anywhere for a while."

"I'll call the doctor," Jack added, "have him come out and take a look. Meanwhile, we'll have Clancy look at your car."

When Jack mentioned Clancy's name, the old man's blue eyes focused on Jack, his injury momentarily compartmentalized. "Clancy Halloway?"

"You know Clancy?"

"He's—he's the reason I'm here."

"Oh?"

"I'm afraid I have bad news for him."

Later that morning, with his forehead iced and bandaged, a steaming cup of tea held wolfishly, Marshall Kitchener offered gracious smiles to Max and the family's long-time friend and servant, Mr. Quigg. Asked about the reason for his visit, the man said he's from the War Department. Asked for his title, he offered cryptically, "Oh, I did a little work for the OSS before it became the CIA."

Increasingly curious, Jack went to check on Clancy who had yet to appear from the guesthouse. At the back of the property, the guesthouse sat like two rustic pine-crafted rooms atop one another. A gravel path led to a wooden porch and screen door. Jack pounded on the door. When no reply came, he entered. The screen door hinges squealed, sounding loud against the hushed stillness of the storm's end.

Clancy was a pilot during the First World War. He then flew privately. He and Jack became friends when a Hollywood production sent them to South America over a decade earlier. They shared many adventures since then, crossed the globe a few times, and Jack loved him like a brother. Some friendships grew so close that one could tell when the other was in trouble; such was the strength of their bond. Jack felt that way now, uneasiness in the pit of his stomach. When calling his name earned no response, Jack pounded on the bedroom door. Seconds later, he barged in.

Clancy was sleeping like a tired old grizzly, his tubby torso climbing and falling, rasps and snorts adding testament to his slumbering state.

Jack almost smiled, until heartbreak hit when he saw a nearly empty bottle of whisky on the hardwood floor. Clancy had a serious problem with alcohol many years before. Jack moved the bottle, and gently awakened his friend.

Clancy first tried to rub the dull pain from his head, then ran his tongue over dry lips, and scrunched up his face. Before long, it hit him, his reason for feeling as though he'd been hammered with a mallet all night. His eyes opened. Abruptly, he heaved himself up from the bed and stood, shoulders slumped, facing away from Jack.

"Something troubling you, pal?" Jack asked.

"I'm sorry."

"What made you go back?"

Clancy shuffled, turned to his friend, and said, "You know what's funny? I don't even know."

"Something bothering you, something I can help with?"

"I don't know what it is." He pulled on the whiskered cheeks of his potato-shaped head, and looked helplessly at Jack. "I was in the store last night, and there it was."

Jack put a hand to Clancy's shoulder. Careful not to further embarrass his friend, he changed the subject. "Ever hear of a man named Marshall Kitchener?"

"Should I know him?"

"He's here, wants to speak to you."

"Me?"

"He's from the War Department, says he's got bad news."

Back in the main house, the kitchen smelled of bacon, coffee, scrambled eggs, buttered biscuits, and potatoes. Clancy met the mysterious Marshall Kitchener and put on a jolly smile as he told him he'd be happy to look at the DeSoto in the afternoon. The slip from sobriety wasn't mentioned, and Jack intended to keep it that way.

After compliments to Max for preparing what seemed nearly a feast, Marshall Kitchener came around to the point of his visit. "A colleague of mine, a man you know quite well," he said to Clancy, "has gone missing, and I fear the worst."

"Who?"

"William Cavanaugh."

Clancy shrank, his stare suspended, focused within. With no strength in his voice, he muttered his old pal's nickname, "Bounce."

The air steadied without movement, until Mr. Quigg, gifted with sensitively guessing a person's needs, brought Clancy a glass of water.

After a long drink, Clancy set the glass down, and asked, "Where?"

"We believe he's in Cairo. We understand he was your friend during the First World War?"

"Friend? He was more than a friend. He was a hero."

"How close were the two of you in recent times?"

"I haven't seen him in many years. We exchanged letters. I knew he was involved in highly classified operations, so I never asked much about what he was doing. Mostly we talked old times."

"You were familiar with his work?"

"Bounce was involved in the intelligence gathering side of things, all the way back thirty years ago."

To Marshall Kitchener, Jack asked, "What makes you fear the worst?"

"He's not the first of our men to go missing in Cairo. All the others were recovered."

"Recovered?"

"Sorry. Not before they were killed."

"How many?" Clancy asked.

"Seventeen. If Billy Cavanaugh is gone, he'll be the eighteenth spy we've lost in Cairo this year."

****

A four-engine Pan America Clipper flew Jack and Clancy from New York to Lisbon. They crossed a sea of robin egg blue, ripping through half a dozen longitude lines, before touching down in the Portuguese capital. With only an evening to explore one of the world's oldest cities, they imagined anxious refugees crowding docks and alleyways, leery of secret police, hoping papers moved quickly through muddled bureaucracy. The war had produced such harrowing days for so many.

The following morning they boarded a ship bound for Egypt. The *MS Vulcania* was an enormous ship, accommodating hundreds of passengers. Italian designed, the cabins and dining hall suggested opulence from an earlier era, a floating palace suited to kings and queens of the Victorian Age. They sailed south to Italy, and then continued on, carving up the Mediterranean at twenty-one knots, on route to Alexandria.

They talked mostly of frivolous things, not wanting to dwell on their chances of uncovering worthwhile leads. Clancy told stories about his old friend, and at one point his face fell, and he muttered, "I wonder how lonely he was. Not an easy life, you know."

"He was fascinated by history, you said. If that's the case, there's not a chance he would go all the way to Cairo without rummaging through whatever old books and manuscripts they might have in their library."

"Sounds reasonable enough as a first place to look," Clancy responded to Jack. "Though I'm not sure how many tourists, as we intend to be, would arrive in such a place, and put a library visit at the top of their list."

"Running around collecting souvenirs for the sake of authenticity could cost a lot of time."

"Jack, if we find Bounce right away, I'll say, 'Terrific, let's go home.' I'm as disappointed as you to be missing Tyler's visit. With Lindy in California and Tyler at Columbia it's been quiet."

Pleased to be of the same mind, Jack quietly said, "They miss you too, Clancy."

After three days, they had their first view of the great and historic port city. The coast curved inward, rimmed by a wide boulevard. Buildings, colored similarly as the sun-blasted sand, stretched over a long distance. Nothing stood tall. Strangely, it was a place where sea met land with obedience. Perhaps it was the scorching sun, diminishing waves to a lazy, placid submission, or perhaps it was the feeling of a single day's insignificance measured against the historical Ptolemys and their generations of high drama. Jack and Clancy were rowed ashore, had passports stamped, and then commenced the five-hour journey by train to Cairo.

On the train, many of the men wore suits and a tarboosh or fez. Packed by all sorts, many smoking brown cigarettes, a dozen languages murmuring in their ears, they chugged through cotton and rice fields. Outside, a boy herded a flock of sheep over low green hills. Clancy slept for a time, lulled by the steady rattling train and ghastly fatigue from so much travel. Eventually, the landscape changed to sand dunes, and Jack awakened his friend when a city appeared in the distance.

Stepping off the train at Ramses Station, in the northern part of the city, Jack and Clancy had yet to feel fully immersed in this ancient land of the Pharaohs. The inspiration of Islamic art and architecture couldn't be missed. However, the hustle and bustle of 20th century cosmopolitan life was visible in the automobiles and clothes, and heard in the loud announcements of arrivals and departures spoken in French, English, and Arabic. People moved with purposeful strides. A Parisian grandeur nearly fooled Jack and Clancy into thinking their purpose was to hobnob with elites at museums and social clubs, rather than identify a spy killer in a place Kipling called, "nothing but a vast graveyard."

A taxi took them south, where narrow streets offered glimpses into hovels and other dwellings. Storefronts were crowded with postcards and fake antiquities. Soon, doorframes took on a teardrop shape. Waves and curls and climbing ridges framed ancient structures. Gilded lattices decorated windows. Arabic markings were seen without French translation, some of which were carved into the weather-beaten stone and inlaid with gold. The occasional minaret soared upwards as crumbling buildings over dank alleyways parted.

The driver put a Lucky Strike to his lips, turned sharply a few times—where was he going?—and then pressed faster as the avenue expanded beneath lampposts and tall sprouting palms. Gardens and wide sidewalks opened the city to harsh sunlight, yet Jack welcomed the European-style elegance. Horse-drawn carriages trotted alongside gleaming Bentleys and Rolls Royces, and then at Ibrahim Pasha Street, at long last, they saw their destination.

"Praise be to Allah," Clancy said.

Shepheard's Hotel, often compared to The Grand in Rome, or The Ritz in Paris, was the pre-eminent hotel in all of Egypt. It was built on land where Napoleon once had his headquarters. The front of Shepheard's was every bit as crowded as the train station. A long-gowned attendant seized their luggage. Pith helmets and tinted glasses mixed with tarbooshes, headscarves, hijabs, and fedoras. Some women wore large stylish hats to keep their skin milky white. Stone sphinxes guarded the veranda where guests sat in wicker chairs sipping ice-filled drinks.

Inside, a hotel orchestra played. Pillars and palm trees reached for the ceilings, painted to resemble the interiors of ancient tombs. Intricate designs had a dizzying, hypnotic effect, anchored by thick Persian rugs. The enchanting spell the place cast caused Jack and Clancy to momentarily lose their porter. Their eyes were transfixed by an enormous multi-colored glass dome raining sunlight on the exotic display before them.

Jack and Clancy decided to eat an early and hearty dinner, clean up, and get some sleep. In the morning they would visit the library. When Jack arrived in his room, he heard the lilting and sonorous call of the muezzin summoning the faithful to prayer. Entranced by the beautiful cries, Jack felt a strange peacefulness and wondered how long it would last.

****

Clancy's troubled state weighed heavily on Jack. He thought back to recent days, when they first learned Billy Cavanaugh was missing. Hunched over, hands in the greasy maze of mechanical parts beneath the hood of Marshall Kitchener's DeSoto, Clancy grumbled about a cylinder bore, a main bearing on a crankshaft, and something about tie rods.

Scratching his head, understanding none of this, Jack said at the time, "Sounds like you're on top of it."

Clancy looked up, his wounded expression causing Jack to wonder if maybe he'd inadvertently insulted his friend. Turning away from Jack, Clancy abruptly launched a wrench like an outfielder trying to nail a runner from third. Surprised and confused, Jack only watched—he'd never seen such behavior from his friend—and then Clancy's back trembled, and shoulders shook. Was he crying?

From a pocket, Clancy pulled a blackened rag and blew his nose. Jack tried thinking of a way to console him. The day had been difficult. The storm passed, but the sky opened to miserably hot sunshine and humidity. Blinding brightness poured from passing heavens, indifferent to grief. Jack put a steady hand to Clancy's shoulder, and said, "You know Max and I think the world of you."

Licking tears, Clancy shook his head, tried to explain, but emotion kept grabbing his words, choking his ability to speak. "I'm—I'm—I'm falling apart, Jack," he stuttered.

"They haven't found him yet, Clancy. He's probably still alive. He's been escaping dangerous situations for decades."

Clancy spit a wad of snot in the grass, and again blew his nose. "It's not just that."

"What is it?"

"I've spent twenty years monkeying around with mechanical parts, fixing things, fixing things that are easy to fix if you have the tools. I don't know, Jack. I just feel so … I don't know, I can't explain it. I wish I had someone, someone special, you know. Why didn't I ever get married? I'm not going to live forever." His face scrunched up again, and he wiped tears with greasy fat hands. "What've I been doing with my life?"

Jack often felt he was the luckiest person in the world. As a matter of course, he lacked answers to his friend's loneliness. He felt helpless. Wishing to offer comfort, he handed Clancy a clean handkerchief, and said, "You'll feel better tomorrow, pal."

Jack left Clancy for a time. He was worried. He couldn't remember his friend being so upset. Returning to the house, he told Max, Marshall Kitchener, and Mr. Quigg, he thought it would be a swell idea to spend the evening outside under the stars in front of a bonfire. They'd all encourage Clancy to tell stories about Bounce.

They all liked the idea, and as Max went to the store, Jack marched off to collect dry wood from the stables. "How'd you fair in the thunder?" he asked the horses. "Nothing too frightening, I hope?" He never actually saw the horses change behavior during a storm; nonetheless, he wanted them to know he was concerned.

While Jack was busy with that, Mr. Quigg, wearing an apron, barbecued salted chicken halves over a pit. Using a long-handled basting brush, he dappled melted butter over every inch, turning them repeatedly as they browned. Max returned from the store with more eggs. She made potato salad, assisted by an obviously enchanted and freshly bandaged Marshall Kitchener. Before long, the world turned. A warm star-filled darkness swept the heavens. Clancy had cleaned up. His chubby face, warmed by firelight, smiled again, and Jack believed he could see some of his friend's grief dissipating.

"He had a beer with Collarusso when he caught him," Clancy said, revisiting a story he was told three decades earlier, "bought him a few rounds actually."

"Really?" Marshall Kitchener asked. "He didn't tell me."

"Who was Collarusso?" Max asked.

"British planes carrying experimental test weapons were disappearing," Clancy said. "The Secret Service was baffled. They knew they had a leak within. What they couldn't figure out was how invisible hands seemed to pull their planes from the skies. Collarusso was a circus performer. I heard of him as a kid. Years passed. He was older, not working much, more than a little bitter about it. He was an Italian who offered his services to the Germans. He would fly higher than the plane that had the test weapons and jump. He'd miraculously land on the plane beneath him, throw the pilot out, and then fly the plane to where the Germans were waiting for him."

"That's hard to believe," Max said.

"And yet he did it. Of course, he had a parachute in case he missed the plane beneath him."

"How many times did he do this?"

"Well, some said ten or twelve times, but I think the real number was more like four or five."

With dinner long past, Marshall Kitchener had a cigarette burning. He let go a plume of smoke from his fire-lit face, and said with a voice that reminded Jack of some of the stage personalities he knew during his Hollywood years, "Did you know that before going to Europe, Billy was spying on von Eckardt, who he knew was reaching out to Carranza in Mexico?"

"Sure," Clancy answered, "he loved those early days in Mexico. Did he tell you about Lenin and the train from Switzerland?"

"I think I heard something about it," Marshall Kitchener replied good-naturedly.

"Lenin was living in exile in Switzerland. The Germans decided to send him home on a train with over ten million dollars in order to fund Lenin's revolution against the Czars. Bounce, disguised as a German, got on the train and stole the ten million. Unfortunately, he got caught and thrown in a Russian prison. But then, typical of Bounce, he escaped."

"During the German's march to Rotterdam—this was of course during the Second World War—Billy was tasked with slowing the advancement," Marshall Kitchener said. "He came up with a plan to enlist Dutch communists. Billy wanted them to stage an uprising to prevent road access. He, therefore, took a letter to the communists' leader. A day later, he discovered the leader was recently removed, and he had delivered the letter to the wrong guy. Billy assumed that, though this man would be better off supporting the Allies, he would be unable to think past the possible short-term gain of handing the letter to the Germans. So, what does he do? Well, Billy had a friend who worked at a local newspaper. Billy put on an SS uniform, had himself photographed, and took the photograph to his newspaper friend. They doctored the photo so he was standing alongside a well-known Nazi, and published it with a made up story. The Dutch communists' leader now had photographic evidence suggesting Billy was a double agent. The advancement toward Rotterdam was then halted in order to uncover the identity of this mysterious double agent. Mission accomplished, for a short while at least. Sadly, a sharp wit and clever mind does not always guarantee overall success ... or survival."

Heads hung and for a time there were only the sounds of buzzing crickets and crackling fire as they each solemnly contemplated the probable loss of Clancy's friend. Looking for some way to punctuate their private tribute, Jack said, "Sounds like an extraordinary man."

Marshall Kitchener raised blue eyes to Jack, and said, "I'm a little familiar with your activities in Shanghai from early on in the war."

"Wildly exaggerated," Jack replied.

"Wasn't there another episode in the Central Provinces of India sometime after?"

"Another exaggeration."

"I suspect you're a very capable man, Mr. Hunter. More than you care to admit."

"Why are you here?" Max asked sharply, sounding all of the sudden suspicious of their guest.

Questioning Marshall Kitchener as to his true motives might have been warranted. However, the blunt way in which Max revealed this hint of mistrust caused Jack to feel discomfort. He'd have preferred a little finesse.

"It's nice that you decided to inform Clancy about his friend in person," Max went on, "but I'd imagine someone like you is pretty busy. I'd imagine your priorities would be to prevent the next catastrophe rather than console victims of the last one."

"It's time I got myself off to bed," the elderly Mr. Quigg said. He stood, stretched, offered a fast, "goodnight," and after plucking a few dishes from the lawn, he left.

"Is it possible," Max continued, "that you refused to see a doctor because you didn't want anyone to be able to say you've been here?"

Turning again to Jack, Marshall Kitchener said, "This wife of yours is very quick on the trigger. I salute you."

"Yes, if she worked in your department even Truman would be nervous."

Amused, Marshall Kitchener lit another cigarette. He then sat looking troubled, the pupils of his eyes dancing with dark thoughts. "In all honesty," he said, "the reason I've come is to ask for your help. Something nefarious is going on. Anyone within our department, including myself, who dares go to Cairo, will arrive with a target on his back. We wouldn't ask for you to apprehend anyone, nothing too terribly dangerous. We would just like some eyes on the ground, and it would be especially helpful if those eyes were familiar with Billy Cavanaugh."

"Mister Kitchener," Max bristled, hearing the proposition as yet another reckless overture, "Jack isn't going to Cairo."

"I'll go," Clancy said. He didn't look to anyone when he said it, and then very soberly he added, "I'll go as soon as you can arrange it."

****

That first morning in Cairo, when Jack opened his door for Clancy, an Indian man wearing a long coat, surprised them by rushing in as well. He held carved sandalwood boxes and perfumed silks in his arms. Kneeling, he set them on the carpet, and began unloading jewels from numerous pockets. Politely, Jack expressed disinterest, and gently guided the man back into the hallway, where he could peddle his goods to someone else.

After the man left, Clancy said, "What did he really want, I wonder."

"Let's not lose our heads. For all he knows we're a couple of Canadians on holiday."

"I suppose you're right. We just got here and I'm already feeling like a target. Sorry about that, Jack."

"Perfectly understandable, old boy."

Outside, the sun felt unbearably near. A tram took them south past Ezbekiya Garden. From there, a wide boulevard offered a straight shot to the Cairo Library. Hustling from the heat, they entered a dark, stone structure. It resembled a temple rising on top of tombs. Inside, a young man, who looked more like a water-carrier than a librarian, guided them through an enormous hall of stone walls where soaring arches rose over doorways. Bookshelves were sectioned by subject, the young man explained. Shelves were devoted to history, astronomy, prophets, spiritual knowledge, and alchemy. The librarian spoke with a high warbling voice that echoed within dimly lit windowless rooms.

Jack thought it might be difficult to feign interest in such a place, but the centuries-old scholarly cavern—one could almost imagine shelves with scrolls—inspired curiosity about the works and their surroundings. The young man explained how the books had been collected from mosques and madrasahs from throughout the Islamic world. He talked of caliphs, imams, and princes, and various chroniclers of each, and after an hour the young man's high voice had a tranquilizing effect. His words couldn't escape the stone walls, so the stories danced around, swirling in the cool musty air. Jack saw Clancy's eyelids drooping, and he too felt sleepy, wondering if they should've rested more after so much travel. The number of rooms seemed endless, and except for two other visitors, one reading and one drawing, Jack and Clancy were the only ones there.

At last, Jack said, "Get many Americans in here?"

"No one comes here," the librarian replied.

"No one?"

"Almost no one. On behalf of the library, I thank Allah, the Merciful and Compassionate, for providing me with your visit."

"You've been very gracious," Jack said. "Thank you."

The young librarian put a hand over his heart, bowed, and said, "Peace be with you." With bare feet to the stone floor, he walked away.

Jack and Clancy watched him go, and when he was out of sight, they whispered, aware of how easily sounds traveled in such a place. "What do you think?" Clancy asked.

"He asks no questions."

"Bounce had to come in here. No way he would've missed this place."

"His mission, however, was to be inconspicuous. For all we know, he spent days here disguised as an Arab."

"At some point the mask fell. He was seen, Jack," Clancy said, and then emphatically added, "Someone knows something."

Back home, Jack told Max he couldn't let Clancy go alone and allow him to feel he has no one. He told her that Clancy hadn't been himself lately, that he seemed lonely. Now, with worries rising about the futility of this effort, Jack wondered if his motivation for coming all this way contained some degree of selfishness. Chances were slim of obtaining useful information for Marshall Kitchener. Was there a chance of obtaining anything? How had Clancy rationalized this? Jack wondered. Was this nothing more than a reckless, delusional race back to his youth? What about Jack? Why was Jack willing to miss Tyler's visit? Why was he always leaving one place for another?

"I saw a bookstore near the hotel," Jack said distractedly. "We could try that," he went on, but inside he wondered why, deeper in his past, he had been drawn to Hollywood, where everyone pretended to be someone they weren't. He tried to imagine what it would be like to slip from one identity to another, as Bounce routinely did professionally, and concluded such work might not be so difficult for him.

Chetan Livrés & Café sat on a large avenue, flanked by Moorish arcades. Outside, an elderly merchant sold postcard-size paintings of ancient Egyptian life. The bookstore's neighbors sold wristwatches, pocket-watches, and modern European clothes. A man wearing a linen suit flicked a cigarette to the feet of the merchant before entering. Jack and Clancy followed, finding a charming mess of books overwhelming shelves, climbing walls, and sitting scattered in stacks all over the floor like buildings in a miniature city. They moved carefully through the disorderly maze toward the back where a courtyard allowed patrons to socialize. Coffee and food items were served.

"See anything interesting?" Clancy asked.

"Was he a collector of books or just a reader?"

"Both."

"Then he was here. How about we sample the coffee and get to know the staff?"

Before the next hour passed, Jack and Clancy came to realize that not a single member of the Chetan staff spoke English. The coffee, however, was wonderful. According to a menu at each table, the coffee beans were imported from southern Arabia, ground locally, and blended with cardamom. They also ate from a plate of delicious sweet dates filled with goat cheese. There weren't many of them, and so they discussed what else they might try. They settled on sweet cakes covered with coconut syrup. A second round of coffee came too.

Jack's attention was eventually drawn to a man, seated alone and holding a folded newspaper. The man kept darting eyes at them. The man's suit was rumpled, as though not cleaned in weeks. His stubble was more than a day old. When he noticed Jack watching, he raised his coffee and smiled. Jack returned the stranger's greeting with a smile of his own.

"You are Americans?" he asked in Arabic-accented English.

Jack nodded, offered their first names, and then invited the man to their table. "A great pleasure to meet you," he added. "Your name is …?"

"I am Kalem. You search for something other than books?"

The silk tassel on his tarboosh swayed as he sat, and all his words smelled of decayed teeth. He had a peculiar way of speaking. He shoved words from his mouth without lip movement, and as he did so, his bulging eyes swept the room with unrestrained suspicion.

"What makes you ask?" Jack replied.

"I sorry. I speak foolishly. Do not mind me. You are businessmen?"

"We could be open to business. We'd need someone to make introductions."

"I do not know anyone, not anyone with money." Kalem flattened his palms on the table, leaned in, and spoke in a conspiratorial tone. "Please, do not mistake me. I am not one of the disgruntled who speaks of liberating us from the wealthy English infidels. I am just a simple one, a happy-to-get-along Egyptian." He straightened his back again and nodded, pleased with the definition he offered of himself.

"One of the disgruntled?"

"The revolutionaries. Tired of poverty at the hands of the English. That is what they say."

"I thought Egypt gained independence twenty years ago?" Clancy asked.

"I can only tell you what I am told, of course. I am simple."

"What are you told?"

"Those who speak of revolution talk of unfulfilled promises. That is not all. They say the English turn our wives and daughters into whores. You are not here to help the English?"

"No," Jack said, and his short answer aroused an even more animated state of suspicion in their strange guest.

"I do not take side. I like English. I like everyone. Everyone like me, thanks be to God."

"Would you like one of these sweet cakes?"

"Oh, yes, please," Kalem answered, and then he ate like he hadn't eaten in a month.

Hours later, arriving back at Shepheard's, Jack was disappointed. Nothing had come from the day. Their table guest, Kalem, talked their ears off, mostly about the horrible treatment of native laborers. He called them fellaheen. He said the British imposed martial law in Egypt three years after granting the Egyptians independence. Three years later they forced King Farouk to accept a government favorable to the Allies. It all sounded very interesting, but what could any of it have to do with missing spies? Jack had been foolish to think they'd stumble upon clues remotely valuable to American Intelligence.

Patience was a luxury for the young, Jack felt, finding the wasted time intolerable. There was something about the call to prayer, however, that calmed him, took him away from all that was familiar. Five times a day the skies sang of devotion, and heads lowered in submission. It was a timeless talk, as Jack saw it, between the living and the dead. Each cry opened a pathway to ancient days and nights, and all the damage of the present moment came undone.

For dinner, Jack and Clancy stayed at the hotel, each trying the entrecôte grillée béarnaise, which they found delicious. Jack had a beer. When Clancy ordered the same, Jack said nothing, didn't even raise an eyebrow. Jack was never the type to go about liberally wagging his finger in admonition.

"Hopefully, tomorrow will be more productive," Jack said, after his plate was cleared.

"Maybe this was a mistake," Clancy responded.

"Friendship is important. You're a good friend, Clancy."

With a shrug and a fast shake of his fat cheeks, Clancy reddened with emotion.

Seeing again the vulnerabilities his friend so readily displayed, Jack said, "Remember the time when Tyler painted over that street sign, thought it was funny? Max got angry with him, told him he'd work it off, and then got upset with me because I took it lightly? You went to Tyler and told him you've made mistakes, done dumb things, but you always had to pay for them. Tyler is a fine young man today because you play the part of father to him better than me."

"That boy loves you, Jack, wants to be like you."

"But much of his decency comes from you, and that's what matters more than anything." As Clancy anxiously brushed the back of a hand against the bottom of his face, Jack added, "Clancy, we couldn't get by without you."

Clancy knocked back a last drop from his glass, sighed, and then said, "As a pilot I felt a part of the action, a part of the story, not the person sitting safely in a room somewhere. A tough guy, fighting in the arena, becomes conditioned to a life of fighting, a life that's extraordinary. What happens when the fight stops, Jack? What happens when years go by and there's been nothing extraordinary?"

"Things change, Clancy. Everything changes."

Having retired early, Jack and Clancy felt rested after a repeated night of deep sleep. In the morning, knowing Bounce had been drawn to history, they went to the old quarter, to the narrow streets of the souks. It was a walk that rattled their sensations. To protect from the sun, long stretches of matting created a knotty shadow-grid, blanketing the busy market. Arabs sold silks and spices. Delicious smells wafted from stalls grilling kebabs, peppers, and turmeric. Hard luck types crowded them, drawn to their pale skin, asking from "My Lord" a morsel of bread or piastres.

Shortly before noon, amidst this chaotic jumble, Jack and Clancy heard their names called. Elbowing through the slow-moving masses was Kalem. "It is you," he shouted. "I am shocked."

"What a coincidence," Clancy said. "Do you live around here?"

"Not far."

"There are a million and a half people in this city," Jack said.

Kalem put fingers to the top of his tarboosh, and bowed. "We must thank Allah, the greathearted and unknowable."

"Where are you on your way to?" Jack asked.

"I go or I do not go. It is up to me. I must tell you, I do not wish for you to obtain incorrect impression of my loyalties. I only explain to you yesterday what I have heard others say. It is not what I say."

"We're not on anyone's side, Kalem, just curious travelers."

"I wish to be honest with you. You will find I am forever honest and trustworthy. Let us walk where it is not so crowded."

With Kalem as their guide they weaved through a mix of Persians, Turks, Nubians, and Anatolians. Kalem moved quickly, and they followed for quite some time far beyond the impermeable crowd. They eventually came to a stone wall that stood over fifty feet. Stepping back, Jack saw arches and a great dome. A minaret composed of three stories, the first two square, and the top one circular, reached to the heavens. It was a mausoleum, Kalem informed them, seven-hundred years old.

Leaning into the wall's slim shadow, Kalem then said, "I must tell you, and I am sorry to say, but I worry for your safety."

"Perhaps you're confused as to who we are?" Jack suggested.

"I know who you are by questions you do not ask. You seek a very dangerous man. Assist you, I can, but the cost may be great. The cost may even be your lives."

****

Though reasonable and genuinely big-hearted, Max could also be fiery. She was protective, ferociously so, and Jack had a knack for getting himself into trouble. After two and a half days with Marshall Kitchener, detailed travel arrangements had been prepared for Clancy's journey to Cairo. Max was greatly annoyed that he wouldn't reconsider. When told Jack was going too, she stormed off in a rage.

Jack completely understood her frustration. Nothing was as important to her as family. Tyler was visiting from school in a couple of days, and was bringing a girlfriend Jack and Max had yet to meet. They hadn't seen Tyler since Christmas. Additionally, there was at least some risk. An element of foolhardy adventure could not be denied.

Max stood with arms crossed, the wind playing with her hair. Having spotted her far in the distance from their home, Jack stepped through tall grass, wanting to tell her he'd stay. There was nothing worse than hurting her. The angry conversation earlier remained loud and clear in his head.

"Tyler wanted to tell us all about his professor at Columbia, Wagley or something. He's famous for his anthropological study of Brazil."

"Sounds fascinating."

"It is to him, Jack, and that's what matters. He thinks you'll be impressed by him. You know how he looks up to you."

"I am impressed, and I've told him that."

"Jack, do you really want to break Tyler's heart?"

"Max, Tyler has a girlfriend now. He's preoccupied, believe me. Not thinking about me."

"I know him, Jack. I know him like the back of my hand, and I'm telling you he's bringing her so he can show her off to you. He wants to hear you say how pretty she is."

"All right, Max, look, I hear your concerns. I just think Clancy needs this. I know he does. And I also know he needs a friend with him."

"I don't trust Marshall Kitchener, Jack. Not one bit. He tells these stories about Clancy's friend, and they sound so exciting, and it just feels like manipulation now—"

"I asked for the stories. Telling stories was my idea."

"I have a bad feeling about it, Jack."

"Max, nothing's going to happen. Clancy and I will talk to a few people, probably come home with nothing."

"Then why go?"

"There's a chance we'll find him, or at least find out what happened to him."

Close to her now, feeling their shared history in that vulnerable, tight-lipped face, their fears that one day luck would run out, Jack could only shake his head. He remained torn. For the longest time they said nothing, just stood there in the drifting heat, hearing the sound of summer locusts.

Finally, she said, lifting her eyes to his, "Don't do anything stupid over there."

"Okay."

"Don't try to be smarter than you are."

"Good advice."

"Don't let me go too long without hearing from you."

Jack framed her face with his hands and kissed her. "I love you too," he said. He then kissed her longer, embracing her tightly.

"That felt too much like a final kiss," she said when let go. "Kiss me again, Jack, quickly and easily, as if you'll be gone no more than a few minutes."

CHAPTER TWO

At Kalem's insistence, Jack and Clancy visited the Door of Conquests. Northeast of Shepheard's, it was a gate within a great wall built to protect Cairo in the final years of the 11th century. Beneath colossal remains, scrutinizing in all directions, Clancy made every effort to avoid notice. Perspiration ran down his sun-reddened face. He spotted Jack in the distance, weaving through the crowd. The two friends agreed to meet Kalem; however, they arrived early, separated, and inconspicuously waited.

Kalem mentioned a dangerous man, an agent provocateur, a mischief-maker who hoped to start another war. He couldn't provide much of the man's identity, but claimed to know the man's whereabouts. As well, he talked about an American who disappeared. Kalem recently befriended the American, introduced him to many people, and then never saw the man again. The man was in his twenties, Kalem said, possibly one of the spies working in Cairo prior to Bounce, Jack and Clancy surmised.

Despite the interesting report, Kalem fell short of earning trust. Where he intended to take them, they didn't know. Also, Kalem's motivation was a mystery. Obviously, running into him the day before at the bazaar was no accident. What did he want? Would he come alone? He was an impossible man to read. Answers to questions came muddled in language complications he might've used to his advantage. His suspicions of everyone invited scrutiny of his own character.

Clancy moved questions to the back of his mind while seasonal winds rushed the street, picking up sand. They were warned at Shepheard's; the concierge called them khamseen, and compared them to the fire of a dragon. An Arab man stood as though he owned the great gate, and viewed Clancy as a trespasser. A younger man, also wearing a gown, offered pamphlets to fellow Egyptians.

When one pamphlet fell to the street, Clancy looked to Jack. With a fast shake of his head, Jack advised Clancy not pick it up.

Jack then ducked behind a camel. Seeing this, recognizing what it meant, Clancy spun, and saw Kalem standing before a stone tower. Clancy turned again, to a vendor's stall this time. He rummaged through leather sandals and belts. He waited several minutes, hiding his face, before looking again at the gate.

Their Egyptian friend didn't see them, hadn't moved. He glanced east and west, and showed no sign of agitation. Apparently alone, passing no noticeable signal to anyone, he simply waited, then ten minutes beyond the appointed time, he left.

Jack and Clancy followed, attempting to keep one another in their sights. This was their chance, they felt. What did Kalem know? What were his intentions?

A commotion, some kind of shrieking dervish inside a mosque, distracted Clancy. Sunlight blinded him. Before long, with Jack trailing, Clancy lost their Egyptian friend. He darted into no alleyway, hailed no taxi. He blended in, and after three blocks, vanished.

Catching up, Jack cursed, and said, "Where did he go?"

"He was here. I had him in my sights. He was here, and now he's gone, like a ghost."

Sorely accepting defeat at the imposing remains from before the Crusades, Jack and Clancy headed back toward the modern quarter, closer to Shepheard's, revisiting the Chetan Livrés & Café. Kalem would find them there, they believed. They needed to reconnect. The café was the obvious place for the Egyptian to look.

They had no interest in meeting the dangerous man, they'd tell Kalem. They'd tell him the whole affair made them nervous. They'd fall back on their insistence that they were merely curious travelers, found Kalem charming and mysterious, but had no interest in foolhardy adventures. How might Kalem react to that? they wondered. Would he cough up more information? How determined was Kalem, after all, to entice them into his world?

Jack emptied two cups of coffee, ate nothing. He said little as hours passed. Clancy sensed his friend's impatience. He envied Jack, wished he too could feel the ache of a marooned heart crying out from halfway around the world. He thought back to Catalina Soria in Argentina. Clancy was a young man back then. She was a livewire, something special. Where is she today? he wondered.

They eventually returned to Shepheard's. The day had been a dreadful misuse of time. They'd be back at it tomorrow, Jack said, but his voice had a far off quality that had Clancy wondering if he was abusing his friend's loyalty. "It's not just for me, Jack; it's for those who've risked their lives."

"What?"

"Your efforts, being here. It's greatly appreciated."

"Oh, I know, Clancy. Sure, I know."

Jack smiled and patted Clancy's shoulder, then left. Those who were honored by an acquaintance better than Jack Hunter could only be among the heavenly world, Clancy thought. He was a valiant and truly valued friend. Be that as it may, pensiveness set in immediately after being left alone, and then there was a knock at the door.

"I found Kalem," Jack said, having rushed over only minutes since parting.

The surprise excited Clancy, gave him a much needed knuckling down of his energies, until the expression on Jack's face spoke of distress. Once Jack entered and closed the door, Clancy was struck by a hard chill.

"He's in my room," Jack said grimly. "He's dead."

****

While a slow-moving ceiling fan stirred the balmy night air, Clancy scrutinized Kalem's slumped body. The Egyptian's sweat-stained scarlet tarboosh lay on the floor. His bronze skin turned pinkish. "Must've died here," Clancy muttered. Tugging at the edges of the same suit the Egyptian wore earlier in the day, Clancy noticed a bruise and a tiny dark dot on the back of the neck.

"How do you know?" asked Jack.

"His posture indicates nobody moved him."

Brow furrowed, Jack paced. He felt guilty worrying about accusatory fingers pointing their way while standing next to a dead man. "When did it happen?"

"Some time in the last few hours, I'd say. Given the heat, could've been an hour ago. I just don't know. Poisoned, I'd guess. He came here with someone he trusted. This other person stabbed him in the back and left."

"Why?"

"That's the big question, isn't it?"

"It must've been a fast-acting poison."

"There are poisons that will take a man out in minutes," Clancy stated matter-of-factly.

A thorough search of the room yielded no incriminating evidence. Jack called the Shepheard's manager, and shortly thereafter, they were put in contact with an inspector who requested their presence at the police station. Max mentioned having a bad feeling about this; perhaps she was right, Jack thought. A taxi was hailed. Members of the Egyptian National Police arrived. As Jack and Clancy were taken away, they noticed unease ripple through the leisured class crowd.

Though darkness fell, the station was bright. Ornate lamps hung from high ceilings. A woman wearing a white skirt, white blouse, and wholesome white smile, greeted them. Her skin was copper-brown, beautifully unblemished. She introduced herself as Assistant to the Deputy Minister, Nafrini Wasem. As she led them across a polished marble floor, she expressed her gratitude for their visit.

They walked through a large door of dark oak. Inside, a man stood. Dressed in a sharp Italian suit, Deputy Minister of Public Security Haka Mahmoud had a slight form, large womanly dark eyes, an aquiline nose, and his movements were graceful, giving him a charismatic, screen idol flare. Though Jack liked him, he remained guarded.

After introductions, they sat. Mahmoud lit a cigarette. The woman was quiet, her pleasant face taking on the seriousness of her superior.

The Deputy Minister looked at Jack. "My understanding is, you know nothing about the man found dead in your room?"

"That's right. Terribly shocking. My friend and I have never been here before. Is this the sort of thing that happens here routinely?"

"Most certainly not."

Clancy turned his attention to the woman. "Any idea who did it?"

Not wanting to answer, or perhaps not feeling it was her place to answer, she bit down on her lower lip, and kept her doe-like eyes on the Deputy Minister. After sharply clearing his throat, Mahmoud stole the attention back from his striking assistant. "You are tourists?"

"What else would we be?" Jack answered.

"You are no doubt aware that the Ministry of Interior has an intelligence arm, the SSI. They will take an active role in the investigation, and their work will be thorough."

"Mr. Mahmoud, if there's anything we can offer to help you get to the bottom of this, all you have to do is ask."

Jack noticed a change in the Deputy Minister's eyes, a narrowing of focus, a pot of black coffee behind a blasé pose, as he said, "And the sunken ship of Nazi gold in the Nile, you know nothing of the rumors, I presume?"

Without inflection, Jack said, "No, but I'd like to."

For some time the Deputy Minister watched smoke snake off his burning cigarette. There passed a long awkward silence with his movements as sparing as from a still photograph. He then said, "I wish to keep you safe. In all probability tonight's mishap will reveal itself as an act of violence. It would pain me to see that violence escalated. Without cooperation, however, there's little I can do."

"Mr. Mahmoud, you seem to think we know something we don't."

"Very well. Nafrini will take you back to Shepheard's. They will arrange a new room for you." He didn't stand or offer formal parting words. While leaving, Jack could see the Deputy Minister's wheels spinning, the gears shifting in his brain. He seemed frustrated.

With serious eyes and full dark lips, Nafrini too had a regal look, but when she smiled, thirty years left her face, reflecting a child. Jack and Clancy caught their first real glimpse of this when she drove them in her sprightly Morris Minor straight past Shepheard's. Playfully, mischievously, she said, "You are my hostages now."

Amused by the pleasure she clearly took in being unpredictable, Jack didn't ask about her plans for them. Instead, he said, "Your boss doesn't like us much."

"He is a good, decent man with a difficult job," she replied. Streetlamps warmed her face to sienna orange. She wiggled her automobile through wide boulevards jammed with travelers seeking the comforts of the modern quarter, and she went on, saying, "Egyptians have become accustomed to thinking everyone is trying to intervene in our affairs."

From the backseat, Clancy asked, "What does he suspect we're doing here? On whose behalf does he think we're intervening?"

"You do not find it strange that a man you do not know got into one of your rooms and died? There has to be a reason behind it. I, too, suspect you are working for someone."

"Aren't suspects typically detained in your country?" asked Jack.

"Mr. Mahmoud will be sending someone to Shepheard's to keep an eye on you."

"I see. And I suppose you're taking us to Shepheard's by way of the scenic route?"

"Someone knew you were at Shepheard's. Now you have a new someone looking for you there. Many eyes will be watching your movements. It is not the best place to be."

"So, where are we going?"

"My apartment."

Several blocks north, past the railway station, they slowed on a tree-lined street. Balconies fronting modern buildings peeked from behind darkened branches. Jack wondered if Nafrini was acting alone. Had the Deputy Minister orchestrated this dodging of Shepheard's? Maybe he was playing a game to earn Jack and Clancy's trust.

Once inside, Nafrini opened the balcony door. A warm breeze put life in her gauzy curtains. She had a striped brocade settee, doilies on the tables, nothing with even the slightest hint of masculine taste in her furnishings. An automobile with a siren blaring passed in the street, and then Nafrini asked if they wanted tea.

They graciously accepted, and Clancy said, "I bet you make a wonderful tea."

Jack asked, "Why the interest in protecting us?"

Smiling with her lips pressed together, she said, "You have been here for three days. What did you make of the pyramids?"

"Haven't been to them yet."

"Do you not think that is very interesting? Most who visit Egypt wish to see the pyramids right away."

She stepped out of the room into a kitchen. Jack looked to Clancy, shrugged, silently communicating his befuddlement as to why she brought them to her apartment. There followed some gentle clanging of dishware, the sound of a faucet turned on and off, and then she returned. "The tea will take only a moment. I am a Muslim, and as such, I am afraid I do not have the type of refreshments you might be accustomed to."

"We're not big drinkers."

Shaking chubby cheeks, Clancy confirmed, "It used to be a problem for me, long time ago. Those days are kaput, much better now."

Nafrini further brightened the room, and gestured for them to sit. She stood before them, hands clasped, two thumbs nervously wrestling. The confidence she displayed in the car was gone for some reason. She said nothing for the longest time until well after she carried in a tray, sat, crossed her legs, and let the Indian tea, from a plantation in Assam—Jack was a little familiar with it—pass her lips.

"You are aware of the current difficulties in the Sinai Peninsula and southern Lebanon?"

"Only what's been reported in the newspapers."

"The lack of confidence in King Farouk has become palpable. Military Officers appointed based upon political leanings. Our current leaders do nothing but fatten their bellies while gambling and womanizing. They are indifferent to the Egyptian people's suffering. Many blame the British for unemployment, corruption, poverty, and then see their king kiss the rings of the British. That man who died is a well-known revolutionary."

"And you believe he was murdered?"

"I do."

"By who?"

"Someone who wants very much to keep things as they are."

"One of Farouk's people?"

"Perhaps. However, broadly speaking, even I would like to keep things as they are."

"Indifferent to suffering?"

Raising a second sip of tea, Nafrini stopped suddenly, let the steam rise before her, and then gently continued. When she spoke again, her voice neither climbed nor fell, but matched the regal qualities of her features. Straightening her back, and maintaining her untroubled tone, she continued.

"The problem is quite complex. At the very end of the 18th century, Napoleon invaded. No doubt you are aware of this. In addition to his military, he brought scientists, engineers, and scholars. They took back to France, among other items, a copy of a large inscribed stela. Twenty-five years later, a Frenchman deciphered the hieroglyphics, and ancient Egypt came to life. From all over the world, people came, fascinated by the history and the ruler of Egypt at that time, Muhammad Ali, welcomed them. He welcomed Western knowledge and influence. Many of the liberties I enjoy today as an Egyptian woman come from this."

"And the revolutionaries," Clancy said, "blame the British for their suffering and, therefore, want to do away with Western influences."

"Correct."

"What about the Nazi gold?" asked Jack.

"I believe the Deputy Minister mentioned something of it in order to observe your reaction. It is a rumor, nonsense."

"And you're helping us because you think we may have some way to suppress a potential revolution?"

Her face crinkled, and for the first time, Nafrini appeared bothered. "When you put it like that it sounds crazy. I am not so sure the rest of the world realizes how precarious things have become."

"Nafrini, if someone has the wrong idea about us, and if, as a result of this wrong idea, someone died, then that means we're putting you in danger by staying here."

"It is not my plan for you to stay here. I have an uncle who lives in the desert. I will take you to him."

"And Mahmoud?"

"I dropped you off as I was told. What you did after was not my business."

****

Before leaving her apartment, Nafrini changed out of her white suit. Now wearing khakis and riding boots, she looked like someone from Howard Carter's team as they posed with lanterns in a tomb after prying the lid off Egypt's Pharaonic past. Nafrini's cousin, Sedran, lived on the northwest corner of the city. From him they procured three splendid horses, and rode into the desert.

The moon hung close and bright. Jack had never seen it so near. The black of night drooped like a net under the weight of a million stars. Below, the land became a rumpled blanket of blue silk. It was breathtaking. As if stepping into that great Fairbanks picture, the Arabian fairy-tale, they journeyed beyond the realms of 20th century civilization.

As far as they could see were wind-tossed ranges, blue crests, a moonlit expanse of motionless waves. Hooves plunged soft sands; blue tassels swayed from embossed silver bridles. Jack felt a strange attraction to the ancient ways. The tent-dwellers were three hours from Cairo, Nafrini said, but Jack felt the sands of time had turned, and he'd fallen into a different era, one having nothing to do with secret missions and post-war intrigue.

Had this been the path of the missing spies? Who was Nafrini's uncle? While discussing life among the Bedouins, she warned against looking into an Arab tent or even passing too near; for such an act would give the greatest offense. While this seemed polite and proper, an act of respect, was it, however, something else? Were there concerns about what he and Clancy might discover? Had she only cautioned them against returning to Shepheard's in order to steal them away?

When asked for her uncle's name, Nafrini replied, "Abd el Khader Idris bin es Senussi."

"What do we call him?"

"Abd el Khader Idris bin es Senussi."

"And you call him?"

"I call him uncle."

She didn't smile, but Jack sensed her pleasure in the little joke. She had a charming wit. Clancy laughed. Jack took a breath, marshaled his courage, and forged ahead. Trust wasn't easy, but all was lost without it, and there was something about the woman. She was put together well, intelligent, and seemed somehow at the heart of their reason for being in Cairo at this time.

CHAPTER THREE

Seated on the floor with upturned faces, the tent-dwellers offered nothing hospitable to Nafrini's guests. Jack, Clancy, and she had come upon a cluster of tents. Outside, camels were tied together. When Nafrini mentioned her uncle there were subtle stirrings but little excitement. An overhead petrol lamp cast shadows over brooding eyes and into the hollows of high cheekbones. The smell of burning spices filled the air. One man spoke in a language incomprehensible, gesticulating madly all the while. Another got up revealing an immense sword sticking out from behind him like a tail. Nafrini remained composed, with Jack and Clancy silent at her back, and then a man entered with a warm smile.

Nafrini surrendered into a crushing embrace. Khader, as Jack decided to call him, spoke with a voice that rattled the ears of those around. The affection for his niece was clear. He was a giant, easily six-five, richly garbed. Around his waist he had knotted scarves, and from within this wide sash, sprouted the handles of numerous knives and pistols.

After a friendly introduction, Jack and Clancy shook Khader's hand. The gnarled and beastly grip, like that of an old Yankees catcher, suggested a high-spirited history. He then gestured with one of these mighty hands toward a sizzling skillet filled with what Nafrini said was goat's meat. Tension lessened. They were invited to sit among tasseled blankets and oriental rugs. Wives were present but discreet in the world of Islam. Jack saw nothing at all of their faces. He only noticed them when one passed wearing tiny bells sewn into the edges of her upper garment.

Nafrini spoke in Arabic with her uncle, and as he listened, the comforting smile faded. The conversation went on for some time until, abruptly, Khader turned to Jack, and placed a heavy hand on his shoulder, asking, "Why are you here?"

Jack had a feeling that deception in the face of this nomad religionist would be recognized. It was a premonition. From where it came, he wasn't sure. "We're looking for a friend," he said. "He's missing."

Khader's eyes fell. He took a solemn pause, and then stood. With a fist caressing his beard, he paced. "A missing friend. I am sorry to hear," he muttered, while his eyes remained distant and searching.

Clancy took a breath, and said to Nafrini, who reacted with no surprise to the news of their missing friend, "You and your uncle are close."

She went to school in London, spent years away, Nafrini explained to Clancy. Upon returning, she found her father to be very sick, and developed a closeness with her uncle. Privately, Khader was encouraging of articles she wrote for the Egyptian Feminist Union. Continuing softly, as if she might offend someone within the caravan, she spoke of reforms. As she did so, Khader returned to Jack, and said, "It may be that in order to stir up more hatred among revolutionaries, and to draw attention to visiting Americans, this man, Kalem, was murdered by his own."

"What makes you think so?"

"Those who wish to defend the status quo simply do not have the stomach for such a thing. They fight with words, and because they have been in power for some time, and allied with western civilization, they have the arrogance to believe that words alone will be convincing."

Jack pondered the diabolical nature of those to whom Khader referred. How widespread was this group? How dark and secretive? The eyes of Nafrini's uncle sank under the weight of heavy consideration, and then resurfaced. "I will tell you a thing more," he went on. "The revolutionaries have a leader. He is an Egyptian, but he is currently on a studying trip in America. He has been gone two years. He will return to lead the Egyptian people, saying he learned much from United States. He will say he can bring cultures closer together, bring freedoms and lasting partnership with the West. However, all is a lie. The reason he is in your country is to study weakness. What he really believes is not different from that of Mohammad el Mahdi, a man whose hatred of the infidel was fanatical."

"He's the guy who killed Chinese Gordon."

"That is so."

"Does this fellow running around America have a name?"

"His name is Hamadi el-Fakhoury. I have heard from enough people the same story. I believe it is true." Despite the baritone pelted for years by the grit of the desert, Khader could soften his voice, and he did so when he chose to be heard only by Jack. Sounding like a mystic imbued with tragic visions, he whispered, "I worry about Nafrini. She is special."

That they'd penetrated a world of trouble, Jack was now certain. He had accumulated fragments of information for Kitchener, although it wasn't much. Digging deeper, however, could put more than his own life at risk.

Talk eventually turned to King Farouk, with the general consensus he'd become a playboy, a socialite, a buffoon, desperate to please the British. He'd been in power since King Faud's death in 1936. The Egyptians were embarrassed by him. They wanted a leader who reflected discipline and dignity. They wanted strength, not weakness, and Jack wondered about the degree to which Farouk was nothing more than a puppet to the British, and how much that played a role in the depravations of the so-called King. More than once during the conversation, he saw Khader cast doleful eyes his way, and as Jack later tried to sleep, Khader's concern for his niece kept repeating in his head. The stress kept him awake for some time. They'd already seen one death; that was quite enough for one mission, wasn't it? Jack finally succumbed to sleep only after promising himself they'd soon be home, and these entanglements would become nothing more than compelling conversation.

****

Prior to Jack and Clancy leaving Texas, Kitchener detailed some of his background. It came up because Clancy asked. He recruited a young fellow with Standard Oil to scout Arabia a couple of years before the Aqaba adventure. He also discovered the Germans' wish to build a railroad through Syria on behalf of the Turks. He had a colorful history that crossed the globe and back again more than a few times. In 1909 he was one of a contingent that backed the Nicaraguan rebels who deposed President Zelaya. "More than ever, wars will be dependent on the element of surprise," Kitchener said, before Jack and Clancy traveled to Lisbon. "Spies mean everything."

Despite protests from Clancy, they made an early exit from the Bedouins, and galloped back to Cairo before Nafrini awakened. The day was Saturday, and Jack hoped Nafrini would remain with her uncle throughout the weekend. "There's already been one death as a result of us being here, Clancy. I don't want to see another," Jack argued.

Having returned their horses to Sedran, they pushed through the crowded streets of Imbaba, looking for a taxi. The scope of this mission, and the ramifications of such intrigue, were much bigger than Jack realized. Everything was happening too fast. Kalem had mentioned a dangerous man who hoped to start another war. With countries and armies still decimated from the last war, who had the money and resources to start another, and how could Kitchener not have known the extensiveness of this thing?

"We don't even have a name," Clancy said, as they marched side by side. Jack, meanwhile, began to see suspicious eyes shifting within every shadow. The conversation with Kitchener kept needling him. "Kalem mentioned a dangerous man here in Cairo." Clancy went on. "We don't know his name. Nafrini thinks Kalem was poisoned by someone wanting to crush the revolution, her uncle thinks the opposite is true."

"We're attracting problems, Clancy, not solving them. You should've seen the look on Khader's face when he expressed concern about his niece. We're putting her in danger, and he knows it."

"She can make her own choices, Jack."

"And so can we," Jack snapped. "I say we tell Mahmoud what Khader knows, and then maybe we should go home and present our findings to Kitchener."

"If Nafrini wanted the Deputy Minister to have this information, he'd have it."

"Maybe Nafrini feels Mahmoud would prevent the information from getting into the right hands due to the politics, whereas we are the right hands. She dropped this whole thing in our lap, and I'm sorry, Clancy, but I can't see how you and I are prepared to handle it."

"She's putting her faith in us, Jack."

"Because she thinks we're playing a bigger role in this than we are."

"Perhaps we could play a bigger role."

"Don't be ridiculous. We're in over our heads, Clancy. Can't you see that?"

"And what about Bounce?"

"I think it's time you admit you're not here for Bounce, Clancy. You're here for you."

Jack had sympathy for Clancy, could feel the heartache, knew well the restlessness, the longing for a new start, Jack felt that way while married to his first wife, and Nafrini was so beautiful. How could Jack get through to him? How could he convince Clancy the danger was too great? He felt awful accusing Clancy of something so horrible, but the motivation behind such risks needed to be addressed. After saying it, he couldn't look at his friend, couldn't face the hanging, shocked, hurt face, and then he noticed something was wrong, something terribly strange.

Clancy vanished. Had he run off? Where had he gone suddenly? Jack sensed it before he saw it. They were talking, and then he was nowhere. What happened? As Jack was about to turn, he instead saw a reflection up ahead. On a chrome fender, men in Arab dress dragged Clancy, who looked dead, and then a figure rose behind Jack, holding a weapon high above his head.

****

Vaguely, and at irregular intervals, here and gone again, Jack picked up a sketchy awareness of his surroundings. In darkness like the sea at night, he awakened. His back pressed into rock. His dry mouth hardened against an airless sky. Was there sky? He saw no stars. His jacket was rumpled up, cushioning his throbbing head. Someone put him here. He moved a leg, and heard the scraping of his shoe against rock, and then heard his name. A match was lit, and in the small glow he saw Clancy.

"Jack," Clancy repeated, "are you okay? Can you hear me?"

The glistening eyes and warm face sharpened; the voice echoed. Clancy's match burned out, and another quickly blazed. What the heck happened? Jack wondered.

He tried to swallow, but choked instead, and the choking hammered his already dazed and aching head.

A clanging of metal followed, a rattling scampering sound, and then a door opened. A lantern stole the darkness. The room was rock-walled, a cavern, painfully small. Men entered, darkly robed, aggressive in their fast-footed charge. Dried blood held Clancy's head like an opened hand. Stubble had grown by a couple of days. He looked terrible.

"Where are we?" asked Jack.

"I don't know," Clancy answered. "I was out too, for what seemed like forever. I think we're in trouble, Jack."

Behind the man with the lantern were two others. All three wore black gowns and white turbans. A fourth man then entered holding a gun. A scowl lined his face. His cohorts tied Jack and Clancy's hands, and then wrenched both men up onto their feet. The cavern swirled. Light and shadow flittered like cold fire. Jack thought he might be sick.

Along a narrow corridor, ducking and shifting sideways to fit through, the man with the lantern led them. Parched and starving, Jack and Clancy walked a long way. Cut into rock, staircases disappeared in darkness. Were these tombs? Jack wondered. They went on and on interminably. When Jack suffered stronger dizzy spells, they slowed. However, between the four Arabs not a word passed.

What did it mean that he and Clancy were still alive? Jack asked himself. Would they press for Kitchener's name? Who waited for them at the end of this passage? Their destination must have been well known, as Jack noticed no hesitation while passing alternative openings in the solid rock. Who were these guys? What did they want?

Jack thought about Max. He relived the first moment they met. It was on board a Ford Trimotor. She wore a houndstooth riding jacket with scarf. Into his eyes, she steadied a confident, cautious expression. "Maxine Daniels," she said. "Friends call me Max."

Pulling him back from eleven years earlier, the walls brightened. At first, Jack thought the lantern burned with greater intensity. It was something else though. The slim walking space through tall rock curved. Stepping closer, Jack saw the light cast an orange luster, and it quivered.

With a haggard voice, Clancy managed to say, "I'm sorry, Jack."

"Chin up," Jack firmly replied. "We got in this together. We'll get out together."

Rounding the curve, feeling the glow of fires now, the corridor spilled into a cavern. A dozen torches blazed. The sense of an evil presence put a new slug of adrenaline into Jack's nerves. What was going on here? What was this place? Over a massive expanse of subterranean wall was a Nazi flag.

"Nazis," Jack gasped.

The swastika that centered the blood-red flag was twice the size of the man below it. Not an Arab, hands tucked in his pockets, he wore a gray suit, heavy blue turtleneck, and tattered fedora. When he turned to Jack and Clancy, so too did every pair of eyes in the cavern. Brandishing lances, the crowd let loose a blood-curdling cry.

The savage roar was not enough. A burst of lead blasted the rock around Jack and Clancy's feet. The gathering then laughed at their cruelty. Jack saw more guns—submachine guns, rifles, and semi-automatic pistols. Shouted demands and shoving quickly set them near the man presumed to be a Nazi. For a while, the man said nothing. His presence alone stirred up a racket.

He looked beyond his best years, but Jack believed his advanced age and inordinately dull eyes masked deception. He wore a pugnacious, scarred survivor expression. Calmly, he paced with the firelight throwing shadows behind him. The surrounding uproar quieted. When finally he spoke, it was with a German-accent, directed at Jack and Clancy. "Welcome," he said. "We are very curious about you. You have been a joy to watch."

Never had Jack heard a man so capable of affecting pleasantry with such menacing undertones. "Men can more easily change the stories they tell," he went on, "the trade-speak they acquire, than they can wants and desires. Do you know?" Hands clasped behind his back, he perched straight-backed in a military posture. What was he talking about? He sounded like a madman, a blustering, conceited, psychotic ego-maniac. "One day a man in a linen suit and yellow tie wants to purchase carpets for the American market, and a short while later, a more academic-looking gentleman seeks to insure a traveling museum exhibit. Both men are inquisitive of similar topics. Why? Both men like the same coffee at the same time of day. Why? Both men appear lonely and pay for female companionship. Why? We have seen such men, many, too many, over the last months, and we watch them. At some point they vanish." The Nazi paused briefly, and then added with a cruel smile, "Business comes to completion, we assume. Who's to know?"

Jack remained stoic. His heart raced. A strange chant erupted from the Arabs. "Gur-ruh! Gur-ruh! Gur-ruh!" Jack tried to ignore the throaty roar at his back, as the German moved closer in order to be heard.

"Lost souls can sometimes never find a way home. We try to help. We try to find a connection, someone who is perhaps familiar with them, and can point them in the direction of their home. Alas, all have so far remained lost.

Do you know what it is to be a little boy having run from home, unable to find the way back? I think you do."

The German was unhinged. Had he been hiding since the Allied victory in Europe? What did he have to offer these Egyptians? Abruptly, he tossed a sharp nod over a shoulder. A horrifically frail figure stepped from within one of the numerous dark arteries cracking the rim of the cavern. He limped, bedraggled, weak like a man from a dungeon after a prolonged imprisonment. At his back, an Arab shoved him forward.

"I would like very much to introduce you to someone," the Nazi said, "or perhaps he is already a familiar face?"

Chanting intensified. Expectation crackled in the fiery air. Jack never saw the man before. Clancy also remained unmoved. Jack thought again of Max, and the horrible future she could face knowing nothing of his end.

The question came again. "Is the man familiar?"

Unable to concentrate, anger spiking his voice, Jack said, "No," and wondered what was going on here. He had no idea. Had his brain yet to settle from the blow? He couldn't think. His thoughts unraveled, pulled by the voices swirling throughout the cavern.

"Never seen him before," added Clancy.

"A stranger?"

"That's right."

"Never laid eyes on the man before?"

"We just said that."

With a disorienting swiftness, the German reached into a pocket, pulled a pistol, and set it inches from the man's head. A loud crack struck like a whip and echoed. Blood spilled. Slumped to the stone floor, the man's existence slipped away. Decades of accumulated knowledge, sensitivities, hopes, were gone. "Then he is of no use," the Nazi said, as he lowered the smoking gun.

Despite the gruesome display, the chanting erupting into a triumphant cheer, Jack and Clancy continued to stage a false show of indifference. They refused to satisfy with the sight this monster craved. They met his desire for them to tremble, and beg for mercy with nothing but cool detachment. What if the man was Bounce? Jack wondered. It seemed impossible. Would Clancy have been able to maintain such control if the man splayed and bleeding before them was his old friend?

The gun arm lifted again. "I hope one of you may be of use," the German said. This time the pistol was put to Clancy's head.

Panicked, feeling a hatchet bludgeoning his every nerve, Jack stood shocked by the speed of such torment. Clancy looked resigned, half-dead already. Finally, calmly, without blurting it out, Jack said, "I know about the sunken ship of Nazi gold."

The German didn't move, didn't blink, yet something about him changed. Barely perceptible, the shape of his haughty comportment lost air. "Tell me," the German said.

Jack knew his gamble set the German back on his heels for a beautiful second. He carried on, saying, "I know others who know about the gold too, the ones who told me about it."

The pistol, a Walther P-38, was lowered. Teeth were bared. Jack assumed it was a grin, but there was nothing friendly about it. He said something in Arabic, and then he was gone, lost among shadows at the cavern's edge.

For the moment, there was relief. The crushing pressure subsided. How long it would last, Jack didn't know. With hands still tied, Jack and Clancy looked at the dead man. Jack had the uncomfortable feeling their fate would be the same. Soon, they were escorted back along the narrow path to the rock cell from which they were retrieved. Clancy was quiet. As they walked, Jack also said nothing. The barbarity he just witnessed hailed down on his heart and gut to such an extent that every effort at piecing together information ended as soon as it began. The inhumanity was sickening. Nothing made sense. What kind of person could do such a thing? Why had he left so suddenly? How had someone found them on the streets of Imbaba? Had they been betrayed by Nafrini's uncle?

The closing metal door ended the lantern light. The prison again turned blacker than a night without stars. Jack then heard Clancy softly weeping. They'd fallen into a nightmare worse than they could imagine. Had Clancy's silence been the result of guilt for leading them here, or something worse? "Clancy, that man the German killed, was he ...?"

"Yeah."

CHAPTER FOUR

Four years before Jack and Clancy were in Shanghai, Bounce was there running agents into Japan. He'd developed a network of trusted agents to report on Japanese fleet movements. He'd meet them in the bar of the American Club as if they'd just happened to bump into one another, and then encode the report, and transmit it by cable. It was a dangerous business for all involved, and he prided himself on his ability to gauge a person's trustworthiness. Though Clancy never assisted him on any missions, Bounce once referred to his friend as the most trustworthy person he ever knew. Sitting grimly in the dark, Clancy imagined he did everything he could for his friend. Nonetheless, he felt like a terrible disappointment.

On a tray, raisins, almonds, and water appeared through a small rectangular opening at the bottom of the metal door. A hand dropped the meager rations, and slipped back out again. Not knowing when the hand might reappear, they tried to conserve, eating a little at a time.

Jack offered what comforting words he could amidst the many hours since they returned to their cell. He also apologized for suggesting Clancy's reason for being in Cairo was selfish. "I'm the selfish one," Jack said, and to that Clancy confessed, "You weren't far off the mark, old boy." The minor testiness that surfaced in Imbaba was regrettable. Clancy blamed himself. Repeatedly, he offered prayers to God that they'd survive.

Levelheaded guesswork suggested the Nazi was trading weapons for seclusion. Within weeks of the war's end, guards, camp commandants, and members of the Gestapo, were being hunted and arrested. It made sense that the Nazi needed a place to hide, and the weaponry provided to the Arabs was plain to see. A sunken ship of gold, if it existed, was likely added to the bargain. Where were the weapons coming from? Had Rommel left them in El Alamein? Clancy thought about Nafrini and her uncle, and wondered what they were thinking. Nafrini came to know a little more of what they were doing in Cairo. Was she concerned? Was anyone looking for them? Did anyone even know they were missing?

"Do you think he had regrets?"

Jack's question surprised Clancy. They were quiet for so long, and he assumed Jack was trying to think of a way out.

"Bounce? No," answered Clancy without hesitation. "I've told you before, my father and older brother were journalists back in New Jersey. As a pilot I felt a part of the action, a part of the story, and it was exhilarating. Pretty soon, I didn't want to be the person sitting safely in an office somewhere writing about it. I'm sure Bounce was the same."

"Why'd you get out?"

"I saw a lot of killing. It coarsens a fellow. Your wounds heal, but never go away. They scar. Before you know it, you got bunches of them. I started drinking too much. I thought of myself as a tough guy, but there's really nothing tough about me. Bounce, however, was a true tough guy."

"Maybe Bounce wished he'd been living the quiet life."

"Maybe," Clancy acknowledged, really having no idea. "Say, Jack," he went on, "Why do you never talk about your parents? In all the years I've known you, I've heard almost no stories."

"I don't have a lot of stories."

"You lived with your mother for a number of years."

"Yes, that's true."

"Was she a good mother?"

"She was good at getting herself into trouble. You think I'm bad? She'd have made your head spin. We moved around a lot, constantly on the move. Her heart was always open to a new man, especially if he had money."

Clancy wondered whether it was the pitch-black darkness, or the hopelessness of their predicament, that inspired Jack's rare candor about his early life. Shifting his weight, trying to accomplish the impossible task of finding comfort on solid rock, Clancy's heart ached for his friend's past. Strange, he considered, how what's never been mentioned yet ever-present, forever in front of one's eyes, only seems obvious after suddenly rising to the surface. Clancy had little knowledge of the troubles Jack faced in his youth. Having had parents who were constantly on the move, here today gone tomorrow, made sense, he considered.

"Growing up, I thought it was because she wanted to have nice things for herself," Jack continued. "As I got older, it occurred to me that she might've been doing it for me. I don't know. Had she lived longer, I could've asked."

"Did she break your father's heart?"

"I don't know, Clancy. I don't know. She'd tell me stories about my father while I was growing up. My father, the Rough Rider hero, my father, the man of letters, the world traveler—it was all made up, created from stories she read."

"You never met your father?"

"There were a number of men who took on the role for a while, but my real father I never knew. I remember once, after my mother and I made yet another move, I was sent to a new school, and there was confusion about my age. They thought I was older—I was a big kid—and assumed I knew arithmetic I was never exposed to. The teacher called me to step before class to solve some problem she'd written out on the chalkboard. I stood mortified, horribly embarrassed, having no clue how to even try for a correct answer. The teacher started interrogating me about what I learned at my previous school, and that they should have done better with me. I don't recall how, but she eventually figured out I was younger than she thought, and her arithmetic was too advanced for my age. One of the other students, some wisecracker, said out loud, 'No wonder he's so dumb.' Well, I became very angry, and grabbed the closest textbook I could get my hands on, and threw it at this other boy. My outburst got me in trouble, and I was told not to come to school the next day unless my father came with me. I wasn't about to tell the teacher I had no father. Instead, I went home and asked if we could borrow one of the neighbor dads. Mother thought it a splendid idea. She didn't want me to feel bad. A nice man obliged, and I felt grateful. A few days later I came home to find this nice gentleman in the sack with my mother. I think we lasted a month in that town."

"Must've been difficult. I'm sorry, Jack. I had no idea."

"I lost her when I was still too young to ask much about her own childhood, her history. She never talked of her mother and father, so I never asked, but years later, I thought back to those days, and realized, in all the new homes we found, she never put up pictures of her parents. It's so easy to get lost in this world, Clancy. Some people are lost right from the start."

Clancy scratched at a growing beard, and then fell into a state of deep thought. A fatalistic vision stood in the way of his every meditation. Jack quieted, said nothing further. Sadness furnished a room in which they couldn't move. Both gave the feeling of having been taken by the darkness, buried alive. Clancy could say nothing further, unless it acknowledged the obvious, therefore, he remained quiet. After an agonizing stretch of time, sleep overtook him.

****

Hours later, they were in the midst of carrying out a devious plan Jack cooked up. He was unquestionably proud of his plan; however, it presented a heck of a challenge to their physical endurance. With tremendous effort, they broke a stalactite down from above their heads. Clancy removed his tie, and together they hovered over the small rectangular flap in the metal door. After what seemed forever, frozen in position, muscles screaming at them, the time came. The vision of a hand with a tray appeared like a hallucination, a self-deception. Clancy nearly forgot what they were waiting for, nevertheless, when it happened, he lunged.

He saw little, considering the mere smidgeon of firelight coming from the opposite side of the door, but aimed to wrap the man's wrist with his tie. Catching it, he pulled. With the stalactite's pointed tip, Jack walloped, striking the center of an upturned palm. A shriek filled the caverns. "We got him!" Jack shouted. The tray dropped. Together, they trapped the man, Jack leaning his weight over the bludgeoning spike. Judging from ear-splitting cries, the pain was excruciating.

They heard a second voice from outside the cell. Clancy grunted and roared between clenched teeth, feeling the man pulled by the one who just made his presence known. Even in their weakened state, Jack and Clancy were stronger than one man, and after a hard struggle, the pulling from outside stopped. Keys rattled nervously, working the lock, and then the door opened.

An Arab holding keys received a swift kick from Jack. Clancy charged over the injured man, grabbing the still-burning torch from the ground. He swung it at the standing man, and then slammed it into the rock wall, stubbing out the flame. They raced off, swiftly as tired legs would allow, twisting and turning through the cramped space, finding narrow passages by touch. It was a desperate shot in the dark, yet their only hope. After some time they stopped and listened. Distantly, groans and chatter sounded. The voices remained far. There had clearly been no pursuit.

Onward Jack and Clancy moved, having no idea where the tunnels would take them. Clancy felt claustrophobic. "Jack," he whispered, "should I strike my matches?"

Also hushed, Jack replied, "Let's give ourselves more time. The German wants us alive, but I want to make sure we don't go back in that cell."

The elation over their escape diminished, eroded by the difficulty of their present dilemma. Every step, extension of an arm, or leaning forward, met with no range, nowhere to go. When locating a slim shaft, they strained and clawed to climb through. Reversing course in such a space meant crawling backwards. Needled with anxiety, hating every second of this, Clancy regretted his restless, pathetic desire to feel younger, to chase the man he was years earlier.

Despite the guilt and fear gripping him no differently than the rock walls, Clancy continued on, clinging to his great friend's heroics. They climbed and crawled deeper into the pitch black, and as they did, Jack only voiced his certainty that they'd get out eventually, that blue skies would soon be overhead. He expressed no fear. Most likely an effort to distract Clancy from their predicament, he mentioned a horse named Lucky, a good horse, he owned in Hollywood. She'd perform the same stunts over and over. Riding hard, Jack would fire a pistol, shooting blanks, right beside Lucky's ear, and she'd never jump, never stop, never get scared. She was an amazing animal, Jack said. He missed her terribly.

Later, the air became less stifling. Clancy convinced himself he could feel it move, not as a breeze exactly, but a loosening from thickness. As he was about to ask Jack if he felt the same, his friend let out a yelp. He fell. His voice branched out into the distance. Alarmed, Clancy called to him, then cautiously scooted forward.

"Careful, Clancy," Jack said.

"Are you okay?"

"I seem to have banged myself up a bit, but I'm okay. Light one of your matches, if you can."

What they could see from the small glow looked like a crater, a massive depression into which Jack tumbled. Farther out, an inky blackness extended horizontally, creating an eerie field of vision. As Jack moved closer, he informed Clancy it was a large body of water. "Clancy, get down here," he called.

After an awkward slide, Clancy got to his feet, crossed the cavern floor, and struck another match. Catching up to Jack, he said, "What do you suppose it is?"

"Up for a swim?"

"Are you serious?"

"It's a lot of water. My guess is it pours in here from somewhere outside."

With a sting to his fingers, Clancy's match burned out. "I think that was my last one," he said, as their world turned black again.

"This may be our best shot, Clancy."

"What if there are alligators?"

"Let's not worry about what we don't know. C'mon."

Though beat to the point of broken, needing a rest, Clancy followed as Jack blindly waded into the lake. Within the cool water, Clancy kept thinking how bad everything had gotten. He couldn't come to grips with being lost beneath the earth's surface, desperately hoping to find daylight. He closed his eyes for a moment, changing his view in no way at all, and imagined a warm bath at Shepheard's. He then heard Jack dive into the water. He followed right behind, kicking and splashing. They swam for what must've been a hundred yards. Clancy was exhausted, worried about how much longer he could last. Jack, on the other hand—Clancy could decipher his actions from the sounds—was swimming underwater for some distance, and then coming up for air almost like a whale.

"Clancy," he finally called, "how're you doing, old boy?"

Treading water, going nowhere, Clancy replied, "I'm not sure, Jack."

"Go under and look straight out. Tell me what you see."

Clancy let himself sink. When he opened his eyes underwater he thought he saw nothing at first, and then he spotted a dim glow in the far distance, a faint smudge of light. A fighting chance, Clancy thought. His spirit soared. Impossible, nevertheless, Jack found it, the black cat in the coalmine. "I see it!" Clancy shouted, as he came up for air.

"Daylight," Jack said. "A way out of here. Can you make it?"

Lunging onward, Jack and Clancy swam. They raced along the water's surface, saving strength in their lungs, and when they reached what must've been another twenty yards, Jack's movements went silent. He'd gone under. A long time passed with Clancy gently dog-paddling, impatient for Jack's return. When his friend finally surfaced it was only for a moment. He said nothing. He was up with a sudden commotion, and then gone again, leaving Clancy alone in the ominous quiet.

Knowing he couldn't last much longer, Clancy felt a rush of panic. Hundreds of pincers clamped his nerves.

Where was Jack? This maddening test of might had gone far enough. The blindness tormented him. Clancy silently demanded escape, survival with his friend. He wanted more life, but if fate demanded death he prayed it to be his alone.

Surfacing, Jack surprised with a voice that mirrored Clancy's panic. "We need to go back," Jack insisted.

"What about the light?"

"It's gone."

"Gone?"

"I looked everywhere, Clancy. It's not there."

Jack set off in the direction from which they came. With no rallying cry, no trumpeting of fortitude, Clancy knew his friend's spirit had fallen. Utter exhaustion had surely crippled them both. Where would they turn? What would they do? Trailing Jack, circumstances worsened; when Clancy tried raising his arms and kicking his legs, he discovered he had nothing in them. More disastrous than fatigue, his muscles were completely locked. He could barely keep his face above water. "Jack," he called. "I can't make it. I'm done. Go without me."

Just as Clancy went under, Jack hooked him with his right arm, and swam for solid ground with his left. At a snail's pace they began the painfully slow process of putting the deepest waters behind them. Racked with despair, Clancy wept. Flashes of his friend's slumped body streamed. He couldn't lose Jack too. He'd never be able to live with himself. Cursing his paralysis and the pitch-black madness, he wondered how they came to be in such a nightmarish predicament. Was there any escape? "Let me go," Clancy said, with spit-choked emotion. He had to say it, had to insist, yet he knew in his heart Jack would never let go.

Soft splashes, Jack's inching forward, went on and on, and just when Clancy thought it might never end, feet tapped solid ground. Jack, panting uncontrollably, dragged

Clancy from the water's depths. Clancy rolled over, hearing his friend's breaths like drums pounding the air. Without a nickel's worth of strength, nothing visible, no known escape, they stretched out as two spent jumbles of skin and bones. They were half-dead from the effort and had no idea where to go from here.

Clancy saw his life pass before his eyes. He froze it in one spot, felt a beautiful cheek's soft young flesh pressed against his, her small hands in his, and then he engaged in an imaginary conversation.

"Catalina Soria was a pretty little spitfire, voluptuous, short dark hair, wore glasses. She worked in a bookstore called the Literario de Oro in Buenos Aires. Smart, knew about painters, talked politics. A friend of ours was a musician who, a few years later, played with an orchestra called Osvaldo Pugliese. They became popular for a while. We had a wonderful time together, laughed through the days, explored. At night we'd dance the Tango, and I wasn't the fastest or most coordinated, but I loved having her in my arms. Little Catalina. What happened? Well, I was there for eight months. One day I got a telegram saying my father was sick. I went back to New Jersey. I told Catalina I'd return, but never did. I guess I just thought I didn't belong down there. I find myself thinking back a lot on my time with her. She loved for me to take her flying over Argentina. We'd go everywhere. I had no idea that years later I'd look back on it as the best time of my life, Jack."

****

Jack let Clancy sleep. He refused to do so himself. He wanted to keep a handle on time. He'd take another crack at the underwater patch of light once half a day passed. Incapable of seeing, he paced. He jumped up and down. As anxiety brought on by hours of sightless isolation gripped him Jack slipped back in time, felt his wife's hand, heard her voice, and recalled all the dicey moments they'd survived. Life had been a series of lucky breaks for him, and his heart felt full looking back.

Much earlier, Clancy caught a glimpse of his watch before his last match burned out. It was ten-forty-five in the morning. Clancy's watch remained on Texas time, Jack recalled. In Cairo, the time translated to six-forty-five in the evening. Consequently, Jack surmised the dim glow they witnessed could only have been twilight's fading blemish beneath the water's surface. Light was out there. It had to be from the sun. They only needed to wait for it to come up again.

When finally Jack determined enough time had passed, they felt a great deal better, rested, and ready to brave the dark waters a second time. Fiercely determined, they swam far beyond the reaches of solid ground, saying nothing as they went. Clancy remained close, his strength renewed. Given that Cairo was largely a desert, it occurred to Jack they were likely swimming in an underground artery connected to the Nile. Fatigue eventually set in again. They'd been swimming for at least an hour. Both were malnourished. Having gone approximately as far as the day before, Jack felt hesitant about plunging beneath the water's surface. What if he found only darkness?

Hearing Jack's splashing cease, Clancy stopped swimming as well. Nothing needed to be said. Both knew everything depended on this. Setting fear aside, as he'd done many times before, Jack narrowed his focus to the task at hand. After filling his lungs with a hearty breath, he went under.

He saw it right away. Far brighter than the day before, the light had become a beam, a luminous spear piercing the blackness; with the semblance of a flashlight, only massive in its size and intensity. Jack thanked the heavens for lighting their path, and then surfaced with a triumphant call to his friend. "It's a tunnel, an opening of some kind," he said. "Just as I thought. It leads out into a body of water blasted by sunlight."

Galvanized by the discovery, weariness slipping away, they swam on, soon over a glowing gateway. They reached the rock wall above the vent from which the light emanated. They took several breaths. They'd be under for a long time. "Important people are counting on us," Jack said. "Let's not let anyone down." Jack would be lying if he said he wasn't nervous, yet in his heart he knew they'd make it. "Ready?" he asked Clancy.

"Thanks for being my friend, Jack."

"Thank me later. Let's go."

Plummeting deep to the tunnel they went. After entering, they swam faster by grabbing hold of, and then shoving themselves off the sunlit walls. They could see where the path brightened further, and scurried for it. Before escaping the tunnel, Jack's lungs withered, pained for air. Clancy had to be suffering just the same. Nevertheless, they remained together and kept moving forward. Entering a new body of water, they advanced upward, kicking and clambering toward the sun.

A short while later, unbelievably, once again, they couldn't help but question if they were better off. They had sunlight, great blazing gobs of it. The problem was they had little else. The temperature must've been a thousand degrees. Once they were dry, and this occurred with remarkable efficiency, their nasal membranes burned with every intake of breath. Eyeballs ached from the brightness. The worst of it was nothing could be seen for miles, only grim desolation, a valley of scorched sand beneath a range of high crags and giant windswept boulders. A brooding silence crept into their bones. Their clothing hung in tatters. Circumstances assumed the surreal grandeur of a Biblical story. They'd surfaced from the Nile, as Jack guessed they would, although what did it matter? What good would it do them? For hours they walked. Flesh burned. They were starving. Baked earth grasped like the dead at their feet. The permanence of land and mountains shifted to illusion as everything shimmered. Fooled with, they'd become a magic trick, staged to vanish in a flash. Little was said. Every painful step further crushed hope. Jack dreamed away the hours, seeing palm trees swaying in a cool breeze, plums and pomegranates, and Max in a white dress, smiling in the soft delicious air of paradise. Clancy fell. Jack then went to his knees. "Rest," he said. "It's okay." Eventually, stars appeared, and were beautiful, nearly close enough to touch. The night turned strangely cold. Jack's body ached, weakened by a stabbing chill. He lowered himself further, pressed his back to Clancy's. He kept his eyes to the stars until his neck hurt. His face then fell into the sand, and he too surrendered.

CHAPTER FIVE

When night and its stars fell away and morning came, Jack stood over the hot white earth, and wondered if they'd been gifted a miracle. He saw a horse standing next to a tent. Impossible, he thought. Erected during the night as shelter for one, the tent wasn't much more than a propped up blanket and stick. Food and water, however, a sense of direction; these were the hopes that put a determined beat back in Jack's heart.

Surely, the visitor who appeared from nowhere, the one who proved Allah the Merciful could indeed be merciful, possessed some knowledge of their whereabouts. As the Nile famously flows north, Jack and Clancy were able to determine their direction; and yet, where were they? They saw nothing beyond desolate land and river, no tracks in the dirt, no port of call for Thomas Cook's steamboats. To the west, beyond the flatness, pale dunes and golden hillocks climbed and coruscated. The profound stillness offered nothing tranquil. In fact, the tongue-tied earth poked a hole in Jack's spirit.

While Clancy remained dozing, Jack staggered toward the runty tent, imagining the night traveler scrunched up within, most likely asleep. From cracked lips, he spit sand, and then brushed more sand from his whiskers, surprised by the growth of his beard. A full week, perhaps longer, had passed. Bones felt detached from unbending muscles. He only realized how bad off he was once he started walking. He thanked his lucky stars his mind was good. A second later he considered his savior in the distance could be a mirage.

"Hello," he croaked. "Excuse me."

A woman emerged. Though heavily cloaked, he could tell she was beautifully shaped. Taken aback, Jack halted. He offered a friendly wave, and the movement pained his shoulder. When he continued onward, she only stared. That he presented a frightful figure he was certain, and so he tried smiling. Veiled in black, with only her eyes visible, a hand went to the tasseled bridle of her horse. She was nervous. Her empty world had been invaded.

"Hello," Jack said again, this time with a warmer tone. Spreading his arms to the wind-tossed ranges, he shrugged. "My friend and I are lost."

The woman shook her head, indicating she spoke no English. When she ducked back into her tent, Jack closed the gap between them. She returned with a peach.

Fixated on it, Jack's mouth watered. The peach, scrumptiously colored as a Cézanne, flew into the sky, landing in Jack's palm. He bowed, expressing thanks. Sinking his teeth into the soft, juicy peach, he nearly cried. It tasted so good. Hardly a mirage, it was the best peach he'd ever eaten. Before he finished it, she tossed him another, presumably for Clancy, who remained hugging the sand some thirty yards back.

Not finished with her charity, she threw blankets at Jack. An embroidered belt arched through the air. Silk cushions and a clay jar flew past. At that point, the possibility of a miscommunication suggested itself to Jack. Did she think he meant to steal from her? Her actions undoubtedly conveyed hostility. Jack felt terrible. Shaking an opened hand, he pleaded for her to keep her belongings. "I just want to know where we are," he said. "Can you tell me where we are?" Into her tiny tent she vanished. A second later, it collapsed over her. She threw off the blanket and stood straight, raising the stick, positioned for attack.

At this moment Jack noticed a spot of shimmering distance sparkled less. A blur had formed. Within the space of a few moments it became a cloud. As this transformation occurred, the woman turned to it. When she brought her face back, she looked different. She had the puzzle solved, and it played in her favor; Jack could tell by the added confidence in her eyes.

Soon, Jack too knew the source of the smudged horizon. Marauders swooped along the plain. They headed straight for him. Amid swirling dust, above pounding horse-hooves, rang shrill, blood-curdling cries. That nothing was known of his whereabouts now slipped from Jack's mind. He had bigger trouble. With dirt rising, and robes flying, brandished lances whipped up low flares, bursts of reflected light. The sweltering sun, Jack's senseless enemy, not only baked the air, and turned sand to fire, but highlighted the desert brigands thundering toward him.

Jack whirled. Clancy remained face-down. How had he yet to awaken? Spinning again to the woman, Jack rushed to her horse. He leapt upon the beast, and flew toward his friend. "Clancy!" he cried. The woman spouted curses in his wake, though they were barely heard given the clatter of horse-hooves. "Clancy!" Jack repeated desperately. "Wake up!"

With somewhere near two dozen riders gaining on him, Jack stabbed his heels into the belly of the beast between his legs with everything his strength allowed.

Clancy stirred at last. To the warbling, menacing shrieks soaring through the skies, Clancy's eyes snapped open. Seeing Jack, he scrambled to his feet. He raised a fat finger at the oncoming horde.

"I know! I know!" Jack screamed in response.

They felt like they were just over his shoulder, raining down on him, rabid as a pack of angry hounds. Jack extended an open hand to Clancy as he neared. Instinct drove his every effort. He knew they'd never escape. He simply had to try. Death, however near or far, could only be met one way for Jack, and that meant a hell of a fight. Clasping hands, Jack pulled Clancy up. Swiftly, he resumed a similar pace. His pursuers, nonetheless, closed in.

Bone-dry earth echoed the beating it took. Lunging onward, Jack's affection for his sure-footed horse, and its obvious courage on his behalf, rose above his fears, inspired him to charge harder. Clancy held tight. They gave it their all. Nonetheless, hunger, imprisonment, and the inhumanity they'd witnessed, had cost them.

Before long, riders swarmed past and circled. Handsomely colored robes and turbans did nothing to diffuse their menacing presence. Bronzed faces, little seen behind scarves, crowded them. Weakened from the ride, Jack nearly fell from his powerful horse. His eyes ached from the glare. Clancy's tubby body was ripped from the horse, and hit the ground with a dirt-raising thump. Jack dismounted. He stood with fists raised, and saw a disturbing aloofness in the eyes of his adversaries. How could they be so calm? How could there be no rising and falling of their chests? Weren't they winded? During a period of animated gesturing, voicings in a language Jack didn't understand, Clancy caught his breath and sat upright, prompting Jack to lower his fists and help his friend to unsteady legs.

"Sorry, Jack," Clancy muttered. "I seem to attract trouble even when half-dead."

"We'll get through this," Jack replied, but as soon as he said it, a metallic hiss carved the still air. A short sword, roughly the size of a machete, came unsheathed. From behind, thick fingers grabbed Jack's neck, wrapping nearly all the way around like a noose, and shoved him to his knees. The same was done to Clancy. As the swirling clamor became deafening, Jack's inner world went silent. All the adventures he survived, the excitements, the wonders, rushed his mind in an instant, and then from his heart came a vision of the one who completed him. He held

Max, the great love of his life, in his eyes and waited, and then something unforeseen occurred.

The bloodthirsty, celebratory cries switched to confusion. A fist, like a hammer, fell upon Jack's head, grabbed his hair, and forced his bearded face to stare directly into that of a brigand. This brigand lowered a scarf from his face, and revealed himself as Nafrini's uncle.

****

In contemplating the Bedouin's ways, Jack reflected on what he determined to be as strict a code of laws as existed anywhere. Judgements were hasty, but were judgements not hasty everywhere? They returned the woman who mistook Jack for a thief to a man of some importance. This man sat atop a horse, almost hiding it with his ample proportions, surrounded by anxious servants, a white umbrella over his head, and orange-tinted spectacles balanced on his nose. The liveliness that followed gave Jack the sense that Khader's men felt they'd done something good. For the next two days Jack and Clancy lived easily among them. Changing from disheveled suits to Arab robes called djellabas, they felt increasingly comfortable. Khader's people cooked for them, provided each with a shave, and allowed for plenty of rest.

To be among the Muslims as they called to prayer in the desert, especially at sunset, was an absolutely transforming experience. Western skies filled with pinks and oranges, billowing dapples of purple-browns. Washing rituals were performed in the sand, and to the east, a stream of full-throated cries praised Allah's greatness.

After settling in an area called the Al-Fayyum Oasis for two days, a government-issued jeep carrying Nafrini Wasem and Haka Mahmoud appeared. They seemed genuinely pleased to see Jack and Clancy alive. They brought new suits and somehow got the sizes perfect.

"Saved at last," Clancy said, slipping into a pair of clean trousers. "I can't believe it."

Jack also felt greatly relieved, and embraced their new beginning with a full heart. He did, however, experience a moment of hesitation before removing his djellaba, such was the seducement of the exotic.

Khader held up empty waterskins made from cow bladders, fastened them to a camel, and said, "We go to the well." They were willing to do anything Khader asked them to do, and so later, after traveling by twilight, riding the backs of camels with Khader's niece and her boss, they arrived at a spot that, from a distance, looked no different than all the empty land. Jack thought there'd be a sign or marker to indicate the well's location, but it existed without any such beacon, waiting to be used only by those who knew the desert best. They tied the legs of their camels— Khader called it agaling them—and built a fire. The moon became a low-hanging lantern, unbelievably bright. They filled the waterskins, and then faced hours of rest and talk before doubling back in the pre-dawn darkness. Mahmoud, seated cross-legged on a blanket, abruptly turned the conversation from superficial topics when he announced, "Your friend's body turned up."

Clancy's face lowered. He had been in good spirits, more than a little smitten with Khader's niece, and after Jack saw his friend's reaction, he said to the Deputy Minister, "We saw him murdered. It happened right in front of us. A single bullet to the head."

"So I have been told."

"Who's the Nazi?"

Mahmoud lit a cigarette. "Mirko Krüger," he said, with smoke now snaking his movements. He pulled a faded photograph from a breast pocket, and handed it to Jack and Clancy. "After el Khader found you a few days ago, you offered a detailed description of the man," he went on to say. "When Nafrini relayed details to me, I felt it must be him."

Though the man in the photograph was younger, the eyes were unmistakably the same. "That's him," Jack concurred, and then returned the Deputy Minister's photograph.

"What does he want?" Clancy asked. "The war's been over for three years."

"Some things never end," Mahmoud shrugged. "They just change."

"And some things never change," added Nafrini's uncle, his words having greater effect given his striped silk jerd and brooding eyes framed by an ever-present kufiya. "What purpose does this killing serve the revolution? It brings the Americans in to prevent the revolution. The British too will make every effort to prevent disruption from what they are accustomed to."

"Killing a spy sends a message," Mahmoud answered. "It also cuts off the flow of information. Do the Americans know about the numbers of people who support revolution? The British certainly know of pamphlets, but do they know the enthusiasm the Egyptian people have for what is in those pamphlets?"

Things had changed since Jack's first encounter with the Deputy Minister. Gone was the guarded language, the lack of trust. Jack wondered if he'd opened the door to a better relationship when he told Khader that he and Clancy were in Cairo searching for a missing friend. It seemed likely, and if true, given that Mahmoud wasn't present during that conversation, Jack could only conclude that Nafrini and Mahmoud were closer than he'd been led to believe.

"One of our men recognized your friend as Mr. Bradley Morrice," Nafrini said, and it was the first she spoke in some time. Her eyes were downcast. She was pretty, Jack thought. Her hair was so black it shined blue in the moonlight, but there was sadness.

"His real name was Cavanaugh," Clancy replied. "William Cavanaugh. Friends called him Bounce."

"His body was found in a wooded residential area near to the Gezira Sporting Club, a popular place among the British."

"You're sure it's the same guy?" asked Jack.

"The location of the bullet wound corresponds, the height, weight, age, the timing. Previous victims turned up in similarly public places."

"What did the man who works in your department know about him?"

"Very little. He said Mr. Morrice befriended him, and never asked about his business—"

"But fished for things all the same, trust me," Clancy interjected.

"He knew where your friend lived," Nafrini went on. "They would occasionally spend an afternoon drinking coffee and playing chess."

"Have you gone to this apartment?"

"We have," Mahmoud said. "Slipped within one of his many books, a piece of paper was found with strange markings, letters, and numbers that made no sense. Nafrini was able to transmit these to American Intelligence. A man said it was an old code, but they were able to decipher it fairly easily."

"Why an old code?" asked Jack.

Mahmoud shrugged and flicked his cigarette into the night, and then Nafrini offered a guess. "Maybe they broke the code used by the spy captured prior to your friend."

"What did the code reveal?"

"A name. Abdo Shadid," Nafrini said. "A name we did not find familiar. Also a phrase, thus far nothing but a perplexing phrase. 'As the sun god crosses the sky.'"

"Is the man, Abdo Shadid, in Cairo?"

"We were going to try his apartment when a messenger from my uncle arrived, informing us the two of you had been found."

"We appreciate you making us a priority," Clancy said with a smile.

"Your safety is our responsibility," she replied curtly.

"It seems this Krüger fellow is offering arms to an insurrection," Jack said, "and in return he's safely hidden."

Mahmoud agreed with a nod.

Stroking his beard, Khader countered, saying, "A man in hiding does not send messages. Nor does a killer display his victim as a symbol of pride, unless he is foolish, and your Krüger is too old and experienced to be foolish."

A camel moaned. It was a strange sound, like a hoarse person being strangled, and Jack wrapped himself in a blanket. The temperature had been falling rapidly. "Tell us about Krüger," he said with a shiver.

"He spent much of his early career in the Middle East. He immersed himself in the culture, despite remaining a fervently patriotic German," Mahmoud said, as the late hour chipped away his imperious demeanor. He was clearly fatigued. He allowed himself an increasingly casual posture, and even eased his back onto his blanket, pointing his eyes to the stars. "He studied esoteric religions, the occult. He became a mystic, a fanatic, but some believed it nothing more than a pose. Success for him required persuasiveness, so who is to know? He spent much time in Cairo, also Damascus, Aqaba, Bagdad. He was in Istanbul helping to modernize the Ottoman army. Before that, however, at the start of the First World War, he accepted a mission to organize and lead the Persians in a guerrilla war against the British. The German Foreign Office conceived the plan and supplied him with gold, a lot of gold apparently, and the mission received the official stamp of approval from none other than Kaiser Wilhelm II. He had followers. As I said, he was persuasive, could stir men to violence. He was also a liar and an egoist. He believed he could outsmart anyone. Some said he exaggerated the amount of gold he needed to bribe the Persians and kept a good deal of it for himself."

"Nazi gold," said Jack, easily putting the pieces together.

"Yes."

"If a ship of sunken gold was in my possession," Khader said, "I would make sure to never be far from it."

"The caves," Clancy said, and his utterance had such excitement behind it, Jack thought he might leap to his feet. "Where we were. It was right next to the Nile. This Krüger fellow probably never was far from his gold."

"But you didn't see anything?" asked Nafrini.

"That doesn't mean it wasn't there," said Jack.

Mahmoud sat up and lit another cigarette. "This isn't about protecting treasure. Confiscating gold might diminish some of Krüger's influence, but all principal players will remain on stage. Instability will not cease to escalate. The future of Egypt is at stake."

"You don't think it worthwhile to go to the caves?" asked Clancy.

"I may be able to send a few people out there, but our time is better spent in Cairo."

Questions nagged and sleep came slowly. In America, the war felt very much behind them. Elsewhere, residual hostilities remained stubborn. How strange, Jack considered, that while on an overnight errand for something as simple as water, between nothing but blue sand and stars, a small group of people could be compelled to kick around all the knock-down-drag-out squabbling of human affairs. Thoughts eventually turned to Cairo, Abdo Shadid, and the unpredictability of things. Some things, indeed, never change, as Khader had said, and in the land of the ancients, that was easy to believe, yet Jack knew never to count upon the future; nothing was certain.

CHAPTER SIX

From a terrace, Jack looked out over an old quarter near the Citadel. On the street below, an Egyptian police car passed, and then came a street sweeper busy with a broom that barely touched the pavement. A bicyclist's bell rang. The heat refused to move. It was relentless in its efforts to burn people alive. At his back, Mahmoud spoke with a friend, a man he trusted, about Mirko Krüger. He showed him the photograph. His friend was German, and was an Abwehr agent during the war. Nevertheless, he said he knew nothing.

Upon reentering the city, Jack and Mahmoud had split from Nafrini and Clancy. They needed to be inconspicuous in order to avoid another incident like what happened in Imbaba. Jack worried about not having Clancy in his sights, but agreed with the decision. The Nazi obviously knew Jack and Clancy had escaped. Would he look for them? Krüger's location, the desert cave, was now vulnerable, and therefore, Krüger likely left, but just in case, Mahmoud dispatched a dozen officers to the area. He told them nothing about a possible sunken ship of Nazi gold.

Outside his friend's apartment, after Jack got into the passenger seat, Mahmoud woke the engine of his Packard. As he did so, pigeons took to the air. Pulling from a curb, Mahmoud lowered his window, and lit a cigarette. He knew Cairo like the back of his hand. He dodged people in the streets, the faithful in white djellabas making their way to mosques across from the Citadel. Trucks and taxicabs made for an agonizingly slow maze. Avoiding them, Mahmoud zipped through alleys and less congested side streets.

"Will the Americans ever stop sending people?" he asked Jack.

"They want to know what happened to their men."

"Yet it started with one who was not tracing the absence of another. Are the British not enough?"

"I heard a rumor," Jack said, "about an Egyptian in America, studying the country, the people, looking for weaknesses he can exploit once he gains a position of power."

With a somewhat demoralized look, the Deputy Minister said, "I have heard these rumors."

"If you've heard of this fellow, wouldn't it be a safe bet that American Intelligence has heard of him as well?"

"You tell me."

"I'm not in the Intelligence community. I've told you, Clancy was a friend of William Cavanaugh. They served in the First World War together."

"If the Americans know of this man and do nothing, what does that say?"

"I don't know. There's painfully little we know."

"That is the reason for faith," Mahmoud explained. "Faith in the Qur'an. Faith in Allah."

Having slowed, they swerved around a stalled camel truck before regaining speed. Jack wondered if the Deputy Minister's debonair remoteness, his passivity, resulted from a firmness of conviction in his theology. He was distant, seemingly preoccupied with something deep within himself. With a fast flick, he tossed his cigarette, and said, "Hopefully, we will have better luck at the university."

****

Clancy and Nafrini walked alongside crumbling buildings, and then down a dank alleyway before coming to a door. They'd tracked down the man whose name Bounce left in code between the pages of a book. When they heard footsteps in response to her knock, she offered a comforting smile to Clancy. The door opened wide. Abdo Shadid presented himself, showing a curious lack of suspicion.

With humility, Nafrini presented her identification to the man and spoke in Arabic. Clancy's first thought was that the man had a strange bullet-shaped appearance. He was short and compact. He now tried and failed to mask nervousness. Large eyeballs sat restlessly in tired fleshy sockets. After much was said, Nafrini shifted the conversation to English. Abdo spoke like a man who knew a hundred languages, and was uncomfortable with them all. He escorted Nafrini and Clancy to a courtyard at the center of his home. Harsh sunlight cast a glow on cracked walls and wicker peacock chairs.

"We're hoping you can help us," Nafrini said, as they each sat.

"I will surely do what I can."

"Tell us about William Cavanaugh."

"How horribly rude of me. I should have offered coffee. Shall I prepare some?"

"That would be lovely, thank you. However, yours is just one of many reports we have to make today. We only need a moment."

"This man you mention, I do not know this name. Why would I?"

"What about a man named Krüger?"

He swallowed and his forehead lined. "Krüger? I do not know," he said, then shrugged.

"I see," Nafrini said, without moving her head or turning her eyes. Her tone remained reassuring, gentle. "Where do you work?"

"I am seeking employment."

"Where did you work before?"

"I have my own gharza."

"You are new to Cairo?"

"Yes."

"A gharza," Nafrini explained to Clancy, "is a place outside the city where locals meet and socialize for coffee. Many drink coffee and smoke waterpipes. Women are not allowed." Turning back to Abdo, she asked, "Why did you leave?"

Clancy noticed a tightening in Nafrini's voice, quietly dealing with her emotions. He recognized the tendency as something they had in common. Only recently, under the hood of Marshall Kitchener's DeSoto, had he experienced a rare moment of letting his guard down, allowing disappointments and frustrations to be so visible.

He'd analyzed these feelings, but had nothing more than guesses as to where they came from. Despite his affection for his family, he had run away from the life they lived. As a result, any feelings of contentedness could only settle on a foundation of guilt and confusion. For him, he wanted everything to be different. He didn't know why. He moved hard and fast, and drank heavily as a way of putting the brakes on his speed. When he finally sobered he used Jack and Max as a crutch to hold him up. Now, assessing his life in such a way, he wondered if he was falling in love with someone he didn't know, solely because she was a new escape from everything he knew before.

"I have a son who is watching the place for me."

From a large leather shoulder bag, Nafrini pulled a black and white photograph of Kalem after he'd been killed. She handed it to Abdo and said, "Did you know this man?"

"No."

"But you must have known revolutionaries among the fellaheen."

"I am not a young man. I have known all types of people."

"We can protect you."

Slightly exasperated, his voice rose. "Protect me from what? From the people of Egypt? The Egyptian people are on the side of the Brotherhood."

"Is this the future you want for your children? To work with Nazis?"

"The Nazis are gone. They are no more." Abdo punctuated this with an opened hand, palm down, slicing the air horizontally. "We will be standing on our own feet for the first time in many years. That is the promise."

"I suspect that is what the dead man in the photograph believed as well."

"Madame Wasem, if I have committed an offense, I am unaware of it. I do not know these men whose names you bring into my home."

"Your name was found in the apartment of William Cavanaugh after he was murdered."

Abdo stood on short legs, and his sad eyes glistened. "I do not like violence. I do not condone it, ever. I am a peaceful man."

"Then help us."

He paced with his stout body angled forward. Eyes shifted side-to-side, perhaps navigating some darkness in his heart.

"We can protect you," Nafrini repeated.

"There was an American—"

Clancy finally spoke up. "Was his name Bradley Morrice?"

Abdo stopped, his face froze, grief-stricken in the manner of one guilty of some contemptible misdeed. "Him, I knew," he said with difficulty. "I tried to help him with business. Another man asked him questions about recent things in America. Some answers Mr. Morrice did not have." Abdo's breath quickened with emotion he clearly wished not to reveal. "He said he traveled too much to keep aware of such things. This other man—I made introduction—believed that a salesman would be aware of a World Series between New York Yankees and Brooklyn Dodgers."

"And then something happened to Mr. Morrice?" Clancy asked.

"I believe so. I was just helping Mr. Morrice with business." Forcefully shifting despair to hope, he asked, "Do you know what happened?"

"We do not," Nafrini answered. "What was the name of the man you introduced him to? Perhaps we could—"

"I do not wish to be further involved."

"I thought you wanted to help your friend."

"I knew Mr. Morrice, that is all. He was kind. I wish him well."

"You can help him by—"

"I could give you the man's name," Abdo snapped defensively. "You could locate him and gain nothing. He is not important. He is a businessman, spirited by the cause, enough to make accusation against the American so that he may earn praise from leaders within the Brotherhood, people I do not know, and could not give to you, even if it was my desire. I am very little. I am nothing."

"You must—"

"You needed only a moment?" he blurted. Shamefully, he grabbed his face with his hands. "I am sorry. You will forgive me."

Nafrini and Clancy stood to go. "Thank you," she said. "You have been very hospitable." She then spoke to him in Arabic, and he nodded several times. He muttered something finally, something Clancy would've naturally concluded to be a farewell, except for the fact that it startled Nafrini.

Switching to English again, Abdo looked at Clancy and repeated, "I am a man of peace. I do not condone violence, not ever."

****

With a brisk stride, Jack stepped into a grand ornate entry hall beneath a domed building that reached higher than the palm trees. He was at a university in Giza. The pyramids loomed skyward in the hazy distance. He'd seen them as he left Mahmoud parked outside.

After several moments of awkward scrambling to find his way around, he was told he'd need to wait before the head of the engineering department would be available, and the wait got him thinking about how the day had been long, and he missed being with Clancy. The Deputy Minister waited outside because he feared someone might recognize him. Jack had been tasked with attempting to convince the head of engineering that he was an archeologist interested in a sunken ship somewhere along the Nile. He sat on a wood bench, listening to the rhythmic creaking of a ceiling fan, trying to think of things to say to pull off such a deception.

A student finally escorted Jack into an office where a large window brought in the late afternoon light. A man stood from behind a richly carved dark wood desk. He wore a white linen suit, a tarboosh propped upon a gravely lined face, and he walked with a cane. Old books encased in glass climbed high walls. The man stepped softly across an oriental rug passing a globe, statues of animal deities, vases, and other decorative accents that seemed to date back to the world of the pharaohs.

"Mr. Hunter, I presume? I am Professor Nazari."

"Thanks for meeting," Jack replied.

"I am compelled to inform you at the start, Mr. Hunter, that we are not a market. We are an academic institution."

"I just need a few moments."

The professor shook Jack's hand, and gestured to a chair, and then he limped back to his desk. "American?" he asked.

"That's right. In Cairo for the first time."

"I see. You informed my assistant your relic was lost during wartime hostilities."

"That's right."

"Am I correct in understanding that you referred to an underwater excavation?"

"That's right."

"Well, as I implied a moment ago, Mr. Hunter, the university is not in the habit of loaning services to private citizens, Egyptian or otherwise. Where is the location of this relic?"

"For obvious reasons I'd feel more comfortable telling you upon commencement of the job."

"For some reason I am not making myself clear."

"Professor Nazari, please understand, I'm representing a family who lost their son. They'd like something from among his personal belongings. Anything of value, beyond sentimental value to the family, can go to the university."

"Why send you? Why not reach out to us directly?"

"The family prefers to keep their identity confidential. I know what they want. I suppose they trust me."

"What, may I ask, is in it for you, Mr. Hunter?"

"They're obscenely rich. They're paying me a lot of money. I like money, Professor. It's a weakness of mine."

The professor gently scratched at his face. He was contemplative, a clearly intelligent man, who couldn't complete the portrait of the surprising stranger seated before him. "Would your operation call for a shore-based platform equipped to provide for air management, the need for cranes and the like?"

"Just a couple of good guys who know what they're doing, and the gear to do it."

"A salvage operation can be far more complicated than originally conceived. Structures erode over time, break up, scatter. Sediments and other materials can compromise visibility. Depths change. Underwater operations become costly."

"As I've indicated, Professor, money is not going to be a problem."

"When were you hoping to undertake such an operation?"

"Oh, I don't know," Jack said, mindful of the urgency Mirko Krüger must have felt. Jack had referenced the gold right in front of the German. Now that the location of such treasure was in all likelihood exposed, the necessity of quickly utilizing this asset must've become crucial. "Perhaps it's best if you tell me when you are absolutely not available."

"We can assemble a team as early as next week."

"But not before?"

The professor shifted in his chair. The sharp-knuckled hand gripping his cane, twisted it as if he was grinding it into the rug. "Well, Mr. Hunter, it would take some time to gather the right personnel."

"They are local?"

"Yes."

"So, if I wanted to go out in the next couple of days, there'd be no possibility?"

"We have a client who will be utilizing some of our equipment tomorrow."

"And they're your best men?"

"They have only requested equipment, this client. But without the equipment our men will be useless to you."

"Of course."

Supported by his cane, Professor Nazari stood. Jack, smiling, said only that he'd return in a few days. Suspicion lingered in the professor's eyes, and for a brief moment Jack wondered if his ruse had been exposed. However, the two men parted with an awkward twaddle of pleasantry and gratitude.

"We don't have much time," Jack said, returning to the Deputy Minister's Packard. Mahmoud folded a newspaper he'd been reading, and keyed the ignition. The sky dimmed to a deeper blue. In Jack's side mirror, the North Star brightened over the pyramids, and thousands of years seemed to vanish in a flash.

****

Within minutes, Abdo scurried from his home with no belongings, and rushed into a late 1930s Ford. Outside, before seeing his exit, Nafrini revealed what Abdo said to her in Arabic. He'd overheard something, she'd told Clancy, not from foolish chatterers. They were serious men, and the men spoke of a high-profile assassination.

Nafrini and Clancy followed Abdo, heading north in the direction of central Cairo, passing Abdeen Palace and a long line of Rolls Royces, and now, as the Ford swerved east around Ezbekieh Gardens, Nafrini surmised Abdo might be headed for the train station.

"Let's hope not," Clancy said.

"His face revealed great worry. Why disclose such a secret, and then run to the men who are plotting such horror?"

"You think he intends to leave it all behind?"

"I think he is torn, like so many."

Weaving continuously northward as twilight washed the sky royal blue, a silence crept between them. There were things Clancy wished to say, but his tongue was frozen. They stayed on Abdo's tail. It wasn't difficult, as traffic became less congested at day's end. Some of Clancy's fears stemmed from a desire not to break a strange spell he felt he was under with her presence. He didn't want to leave her side, and he didn't want to say anything that could prove divisive. He resolved to be content with the precious moments he had with her, knowing not how long they might last.

"An assassination of King Farouk," Nafrini said, "would turn people against those sympathetic to a revolution."

"Is it possible they're targeting one of the British?"

She grimly shook her head, not answering, not knowing. After more blocks, and a further darkening of the sky, Clancy asked, "If he intends to leave by train, what do we do?"

"We have no choice. We let him."

An hour later, Abdo Shadid was gone. He'd boarded a train bound for Alexandria. Among the chaos of foot-traffic and the booming announcements of arrivals and departures, Nafrini and Clancy had taken their pursuit as far as they could. "I do not doubt him, his information," Nafrini said. "But the Deputy Minister will. It is good we have seen him leave so quickly. It will offer support to the truth of his words."

"What now?"

"The Deputy Minister will want to relay this to his superior and State Security as soon as possible." Marching back to her Morris Minor with Clancy on her heels, she continued. "Perhaps they had luck with the German agent. He has been a good friend. Hopefully he provided information that could help us put pieces together."

Outside Ramses Station, automobiles inched for space. People from all over converged, hustling to various destinations. Nafrini and Clancy pressed through blaring horns and shining fenders to cross into a suburb where she parked.

"Would you mind terribly," Clancy said, catching sight of a dingy café, "if we stop for five minutes, and have a cup of coffee? Just five minutes. I know we're in a hurry, but it's been a very long day." Flustered by the surprise on her face, he waved away the idea with a fast, "Never mind. It's not important. I'll be fine."

"No. I like coffee."

They ducked into a tiny hole-in-the-wall with tables constructed from banged up tin, and few people sat. Old men played backgammon. Smoke rose in sweet-smelling plumes. The café displayed a medieval weariness offset by a colorful French poster. Turkish coffees arrived quickly. "I have been thinking, Clancy. May I call you Clancy?"

"Of course."

She kept her voice to a whisper. "Suppose a terrible thing happened to one of the religious leaders? It would stir greater fanaticism on the part of the Brotherhood."

Clancy shook his head, feeling overwhelmed, and said, "Could you fancy yourself living in America?"

Her eyebrows pinched as she replied, "Why ask such a thing?"

"I don't know. I just want to talk about something else for a moment."

"Well, keep in mind, we only have a moment." She sipped her coffee, holding the glass with both hands, and then said, "In many ways it was an exhilarating experience living in London, but I could not shake the guilt I felt for leaving home."

"I know what that feels like."

"You do?"

"I suspect you and I have more in common than you think."

"Did your mother sprinkle rose water on your friends when they came over?"

"I'm sure she did a great many things you would find unusual. So, you liked living in London?"

"I did. I liked it very much. I lived with a family in close proximity to other families. When I was not studying there seemed to be a never-ending amount of work to do. The women worked hard, washing in metal buckets and tubs, ironing, shopping for the day's food. Men worked seven days before getting one day off. But the smiling and laughing in front of the men made an impression on me. We had a wireless, and a wind-up gramophone. A surprising number of people played musical instruments. The home would become lively and tender. I have wondered many times since if it was the foreign-ness—is that a word?—that appealed to me, or perhaps I found it a better way of living than what I experienced growing up. I have yet to resolve myself to an answer."

Clancy's heart beat like taps on calm water. The ripple effect caused a tingling on his skin. Her chin lowered, and eyes warmed in a way he recognized. Once in a blue moon, if even that, Clancy charmed a beautiful woman, but he hadn't seen such an expression in years.

"You are smiling," she said. "Why are you smiling? You have a nice smile. Do you know that?"

"The world is such a mess. It's comforting to know others feel as you do."

"My uncle would say your anger at the world is really an anger at yourself for foolishly accepting your powerless position in it."

"Your uncle is wise."

"We should not let the world frame the short lives we are given."

CHAPTER SEVEN

Despite the late hour, the Deputy Minister showed no sign of exhaustion. He sat with legs crossed and back straight, thinking. Nafrini also sat quietly composed. Clancy paced, occasionally swinging his arms at his sides. A haze collected around the ornate lamps suspended from the high ceiling. The Deputy Minister had been smoking one cigarette after the next for some time, and there was little movement to jostle the gloom. Slumped and frustrated, Jack kept shifting in his chair, trying to stay awake, failing to piece together what seemed an impossible puzzle.

"I do not believe they would plot to intentionally murder a holy man," Mahmoud said finally. "Sacrificing a foot soldier for the cause is one thing, and we have no solid evidence they have even done that. We are missing something."

"Prince Hassan Hassan," Jack suggested.

"Why?"

"I don't know. He's a public figure."

Abruptly, Mahmoud stood, stubbed out his cigarette, and looked to the room's middle as if something was there. He stared intently for a moment, and then, as if hypnotized, he walked out through the large oak door. Perhaps too tired to speculate on where he went, no one said a word. When he returned a few minutes later, he held the newspaper he had in his car. "Hamadi el-Fakhoury has been in the United States for two years," he said. "All the writings about him express hope that he will be a bridge between nationalists and imperialists. They refer to him as moderate, yet there are murmurings this is not who he is at all, that he is in fact, an anti-imperialist revolutionary. I do not know. None of us know. But let us suppose he is as the rumors say. What would he do to another who is written about in the same manner? Would he willingly stand by and allow a competitor to surface as leader to a reformed Egypt?"

Nafrini leaned forward in her chair. Her eyes swung back and forth, carefully considering Mahmoud's intimation. "Omar Tahan," she said.

Mahmoud tossed the newspaper to his desk, and it landed with a thwack. "Omar Tahan is giving a speech on board one of Thomas Cook's tourist steamers tomorrow. The newspaper describes it as an important speech for the future of the country. Many people will be there, including dignitaries from the West."

"*Death on the Nile*?" Clancy said after the astonishment settled. "It seems too fantastic."

"A high-profile assassination. One for the history books."

"There's only one problem," Jack said. "Professor Nazari's salvage equipment is going out tomorrow. They go after the gold on the same day they pull off a political assassination, both events taking place on the Nile?"

Mahmoud said, "Let us consider what we know—"

"A boat," Nafrini exclaimed with a sudden epiphany. "A boat plays a role in this. 'As the sun god crosses the sky.' Remember? Mr. Cavanaugh wrote it in code. I have been trying to decipher its meaning. The sun god is Ra, and according to ancient Egyptians, Ra traveled across the sky by boat. Boats were of paramount importance to Egyptians. They did everything by boat— fish, travel, hunt, trade, war. Kings were buried with boats; Tutankhamen was buried with thirty-five wooden model boats."

"'As the sun god crosses the sky,' is a warning about this Omar fellow and his speech on a steamer?" Clancy asked, while lowering himself into a leather chair.

"Why else would your friend have made a point of putting such things in code? He provides two pieces of information, Abdo Shadid and this phrase. One informs us of a public assassination, the other informs us of the location where it is to take place."

"Perhaps he was referring to the sunken ship of Nazi gold," Jack said.

"Gold can only support change," Mahmoud said. "It is not the change."

Jack stood and paced. He shook his head, agitated, desperate for sleep. "I don't know," he said. "It just seems so—"

"You remain skeptical?" Mahmoud asked.

"What's difficult to understand is that people aren't tired of conflict. The war ended only three years ago."

"During the war, the British imposed martial law in Egypt. That was three years after the Egyptians gained their theoretical independence. The Egyptian people want their fate to be in the hands of their own, if it also pleases Allah."

Nafrini said, "If el-Fakhoury is behind this and manages to succeed in his task, the Egyptian people will not get to choose, and they deserve to choose."

"What makes you so certain King Farouk's time has passed?"

"His military suffered terrible embarrassment in the Sinai Peninsula. He has lost what little respect he had. Everyone knows his days are numbered."

"Of course, I would never argue against taking the cautionary approach," Clancy said, as he sat with stubby fingers stroking his chin.

Jack concurred. "I suppose the prudent thing would be to go to the Cook touring company in the morning, and quietly present our case to Omar Tahan."

"The steamers take days traveling the Nile. He has likely already gone."

"Can we catch up to it?"

"What if the assassination is more than an assassination?" Clancy supposed. "What I mean is—what if the assassination acts as a marker? What if the trigger is pulled directly above where the gold rests at the bottom of the Nile?"

"Too fanciful," the Deputy Minister said.

"Well, the whole thing is outrageous, isn't it? You said 'one for the history books.' I thought they wanted to make a big show of things."

"Your theory risks too many extraneous factors. What if Omar Tahan is sleeping, and he has a guard at his door at the exact time they sail over the lost German ship?"

"I didn't think about that," Clancy muttered softly.

"The assassination is, aside from removing a political opponent, about drama, theater, and inciting terror, so that someone can rise above it, claim to be reasonable, and offer a return to order," Mahmoud stated. "I believe the assassination will take place either during the speech or directly after. And if Mirko Krüger is involved, you can be certain nothing is left to chance."

****

Impatient for morning, Jack rubbed fatigue from his eyes. Improbable scenarios, alternative ones, were passed around the room, batted back and forth, and shot down for various reasons, until Mahmoud pulled reference materials in order to scrutinize the logistics of such an operation. He could have simply telephoned the three ships and asked about the presence of Omar Tahan, but he considered that a conspiracy could be more far-reaching than he knew, and therefore decided against taking the chance.

At one point, Jack asked the Deputy Minister if he thought it wise to get the Interior Minister involved, and was surprised by the agitation he witnessed as a result. Mahmoud explained that the Interior Minister was more of a figurehead. He was not Egyptian, and did very little aside from hobnob with elites. "He is duty bound only to debauchery," the Deputy Minister said, "but you did not hear that from me."

"It would've been nice if the newspaper had offered the name of the steamer Tahan is sailing on," Jack said.

"Perhaps the newspaper is a conspirator as well," Clancy mumbled in response.

A Nile voyage lasted three weeks. It was an enormously popular thing to do among the wealthiest who flocked to Egypt in the late nineteenth century. War and economic troubles had changed everything. Over time, Thomas Cook's fleet of luxury cruisers was greatly reduced. Fortunately, the Deputy Minister had a schedule for the remaining steamers that carried tourists into the ancient past. In two days, the *Delta* was to disembark, which removed that steamer as a possibility. That left the *Arabia*, the *Ibis*, or the *Sudan*. These were leisurely expeditions, hardly fast ships, and in that, Jack and his friends found their only advantage.

There were many stops along the way. The first was in Badrashin. However, all three steamers would be beyond that point, given that it was a scheduled stop on the same day the tours commenced, and none were scheduled to commence the coming morning. The next stop was Ayat, then Gebel al-Deir, followed by Beni Hasan. Passengers then went to Asyut. That was followed by Qena, and then Karnak and Luxor, until finally, Aswan.

Cairo to Ayat was thirty miles. Moving upstream at fifteen miles per hour, the steamers were clearly beyond that point as well. Looking up from maps and date books,

Jack said, "Assuming nothing has changed, the *Ibis* left fifteen days ago."

"Then it is returning to Cairo," Mahmoud replied.

"Giving a speech at the end of the tour could make sense, but it also runs risks," Jack reasoned. "Passengers have seen extraordinary ruins that date back thousands of years. Even a great speaker could be boring after such marvels of history."

Following Jack's logic, Clancy said, "Passengers could also be tired, anxious to return, distracted."

"A sensible conjecture," Mahmoud agreed.

"Cairo to Gebel al-Deir is one hundred and twenty-five miles," Jack said, "and Beni Hasan is twice that distance. The *Arabia*, according to your schedule here, is the most recent departure, and has been gone only five days. Given the amount of time tourists spend at each location, the cruising speed of the steamers, and my continued scrutiny of these maps and dates of departures, Beni Hasan seems our best bet. We can get there by car in five hours. The sun will be just coming up. Something about it feels right. There are temples and tombs cut into cliffs. Perhaps significantly, it served ancient Egypt as a cemetery site."

Blaring loudly against the late night intimacy, a telephone rang. Nafrini answered. While listening, her face noticeably tensed. "He is here with me," she said, looking to the Deputy Minister. "An officer from Soliman Pasha," she said, upon ending the call. "He tried reaching you at your home. He said there is a riot. A fire has been started in Gresham Court. People are waving signs and shouting."

While the ramifications of such a thing stirred in his head, the Deputy Minister pinched his temples with a thumb and forefinger, and then slumped in a chair. "So much is happening at once," he snarled.

"It's connected," Jack said, "has to be. Start a riot to preoccupy law enforcement. It sounds like the type of thing they do."

"My job is to see things before they happen. I have sent many officers just north of Dendara where Krüger held you captive. I have been a fool." His open hands ran down his face, and the weariness nearly gave him the appearance of a different man. "I have stretched the department too thin."

"Someone could be informing Mirko Krüger of your actions," Jack suggested.

"It is possible."

"An officer here in Cairo could have a friend in the department who is in Dendara right now, and he knows why his friend is in Dendara. A simple telephone call from this fellow and the match is lit."

"Very true," muttered the Deputy Minister.

He then did something unexpected. He took Nafrini's hand. She had been standing next to him. As he gently clasped his fingers around hers, his affection was clear. There was something between them, and the Deputy Minister had only just now felt comfortable enough with Jack and Clancy to reveal it.

Jack shifted his gaze to Clancy, who stood stupidly with his mouth open. His face hung like a wet sock. Had Nafrini somehow missed Clancy's feelings? Why hadn't she told him of this relationship? "So, we go after the *Arabia*?" Jack said, returning to their most urgent dilemma.

"At Beni Hasan, yes," the Deputy Minister replied. "Let us hope Omar Tahan is not traveling on the *Sudan*. I will send what number of officers can be afforded."

"You can't trust your officers," Jack fired back. "You just acknowledged that."

Mahmoud abruptly stood and paced. "I do not think you understand. There is a riot down the street. It is real. It is not a theory. I must do my job to put it down. If there is any excuse to replace me, it will be used, and I will be out of a job. You will not go alone."

"I will go," Nafrini said.

"It is too dangerous."

"Like you, my responsibility is to law enforcement."

"No."

"You're giving them what they want," Jack said. "They had ideas about how they might manipulate you, and you're allowing it to happen exactly as they planned."

Nafrini put a delicate hand on Mahmoud's arm, and said, "Will you allow the extremists a victory in order to save your job? We need to stop this."

Mahmoud stared at the polished floor, hands pensively placed at his hips. "Do what you must," he said, and then his eyes lifted to Nafrini, and he added, "Be careful."

CHAPTER EIGHT

Washed in blue silver beneath stars, south along the Nile, were canals and drains, some of them twenty meters wide. Concrete became dusty desert road. Occasionally, Nafrini navigated camel trails. While driving, she talked of what to expect. The *Arabia* would be at Beni Hasan, moored overnight. After breakfast, passengers would travel to the ruins. There would be dragomen, donkey boys, and curio sellers. Clancy half-listened. He couldn't shake the vision of her holding hands with Mahmoud.

What did he expect? She reported to a handsome, debonair figure of some importance, a man closer to her age. Other men too probably longed for her, men who also shared her heritage and culture. What was Clancy thinking? He was such an idiot; she was so beautiful, refined, and intelligent. What interest could she possibly have in a tubby fool like him?

Clancy closed his eyes for a while, and escaped into his past, shoved all the troubles away. He'd been quite the daredevil during the First World War. No matter how much his thinking occasionally tilted toward self-pity, he always felt lucky to look back on those days. At pubs in villages, drinking with fellow flyers, toasting their survival, he never felt as alive as in the hours after a near death experience. He was so young at the time, he reflected, not much more than a kid.

"I wish Bounce was here," he mumbled, feeling exhausted. His friend got his nickname because nobody could take him down. He was indestructible. Clancy rubbed his eyes, and in doing so, tried to remove memories from his worn out brain. He noticed the sky glowed brighter. What happened to the time?

The speech was scheduled for evening. Many hours remained. Jack wondered out loud if Professor Nazari's diving equipment wasn't for the gold after all; perhaps it would be used only to get aboard the steamer. Their biggest worry was that Omar Tahan might not tour the ruins. If he decided to remain on the *Arabia*—he might prefer to practice his speech—what would they do? How would they get to him?

"We seem to be getting close," Jack said.

"We will be there with no time to spare," Nafrini replied.

Soon the Nile spread out before them. Next to a black jetty extending from the shore, a signpost read *Thomas Cook & Son*. Beyond that, a beautiful double-decked steamer rested. At its center, in bold capital letters, was the name *Arabia*. Straight-backed stewards in red tarbooshes and long white djellabas moved about in service of the guests. The immense waters below reflected the morning's somber light.

Nafrini had visited these ruins before. She guided them along a steep flight of stone steps in the west-facing cliff-side. Upon reaching the top, the Nile Valley came into view. Even more spectacular than the vast desert and river below were the tombs carved directly into the limestone hills. Tall pillars fronted deep recesses. The site was far more imposing than Clancy anticipated.

From seemingly nowhere a man stepped forward. He wore a suit, and introduced himself as an officer from the antiquities services. Sand on his nose and forehead indicated he'd said his morning prayers. Nafrini spoke to him in Arabic, identifying herself as Assistant Deputy Minister, and explained she was tasked with offering a tour to the Americans. The man lit a thin brown cigarette and bowed his head in a show of modesty before walking away.

Once inside, they were met with surprisingly spacious tombs cut with ceilings flat and walls at ninety-degree angles. Ancient paintings with beautifully and intricately composed rhythmic shapes, not unlike wallpaper, covered the stone, depicting hunting, fishing, and battle scenes. Nafrini explained that one wall depicted a funerary scene with the deceased dragged on a sledge into the tomb where they presently stood. The painted scenes and relief sculpture acted as biographical text.

Hearing noise from an approaching crowd, Jack and Clancy backed into shadows. Undoubtedly, they were the *Arabia* passengers. A hush came over them as they entered. Their eyes scanned the marvels along the walls. Clearly an international lot, they whispered in many languages. There didn't seem to be a suspicious one among them. Some of the men wore Panama hats and suspenders, some linen suits. Women wore high waist, wide leg trousers, or slinky polka dot dresses. They examined walls and statues like newly schooled Egyptologists.

Their dragoman was draped in colors more theatrical than the servants who remained aboard the *Arabia*. With grand gestures he elucidated on how the ruins became a passport into the ancient Egyptian mind. "Many Egyptians believed the decorations guaranteed a continuation of life, and from a certain point of view, they were right."

"See Omar Tahan?" Clancy quietly asked, as he left Jack, and stepped to Nafrini's side.

"I do not," she whispered.

"I suppose if Krüger's part of this bunch he'd stay on the boat. What do we do? Do we know the location of the other steamer?"

"We might ask someone if Omar Tahan is with this tour."

While Nafrini continued scrutinizing the crowd, Clancy's eyes lowered to the stone floor. He dragged the edge of his shoe against rock, and then whispered, "It didn't escape my notice that you and the Deputy Minister seem to be close, more than colleagues, I mean."

She allowed for a long time before replying, and then finally whispered in return, "He has asked me to marry him."

"I would qualify that as—" He stammered, caught with emotion, and then continued, "I'd say that's a relationship beyond professional. Congratulations." Taking a fast glance, he saw her lips tighten, her face warmed by a nearby light meant for stone. She was perhaps the most beautiful woman he'd ever seen. "Nafrini, I hope you'll take this the right way. I certainly don't mean any offense. I just want to say that I hope he's wonderful to you. You deserve someone like that. Every day should—every day should, for him, be a new mission to make you happy."

"I still have not answered him," she said.

"So, I still have a shot? Sorry. I don't mean to—"

"I like you, Clancy. You have a kind heart. I would love for you to show me America. Mahmoud is traditional. And I wish to be part of a world that is more forward thinking."

"Why allow him to hold your hand? Why not just tell him?"

"It is not that simple. He is a good man. It is all so confusing. And I feel torn. I am tired of feeling torn. I wish for easy answers where there are none."

"It would make me ridiculously happy to know there's a remote possibility you might consider holding my hand one day."

She bit down on her lip. "I would like that," she whispered. She then sighed, and ended the conversation, saying, "But not today."

Clancy watched her turn and slip through the crowd. The tall dark dragoman continued with his oration, holding the tourists spellbound, and Clancy regretted his clumsiness. Why hadn't he waited? She probably found him impulsive, inappropriately so.

A light shove pressed against Clancy's back. He turned and saw no one. He thought Jack had come up behind him. In the spot where he felt the nudge, he now experienced a strain, and it throbbed. The pain rapidly worsened, nearly sending him to his knees. He reached back and set a palm against the hurt. His shirt was wet. For the briefest of moments he thought someone spilled water on him. However, when he brought his hand back around and looked at it, he realized the wetness came from beneath his skin. He became light-headed, but not so confused as to be unaware he'd been stabbed.

As he collapsed, the stone floor snapped his wrist. This second hammering of pain caused him to roll over. Ghastly screams filled the chamber. Though already on the floor, Clancy felt his weight falling and he thought he might get sick, and then everything went black.

****

Jack sank his heels into a horse's flanks, and flew along the eastern bank of the Nile. The vision of Clancy on the ground with blood pouring out of him surfaced over and over in Jack's mind. No one saw who did it. Jack had been outside. Donkey boys had arrived hoping to hustle rides to tourists weary of too much walking. Once screams died, the dragoman herded everyone to the steamer for their safety. Bedouins came; one gave Jack his horse, while Nafrini raced to Cairo with Clancy in her Morris Minor. It all happened so fast. Jack felt rage, an overwhelming hatred. It was anger beyond anything he experienced before.

The horse, a chestnut-colored Arabian, reminded him of Lucky. She was another hot-blooded breed, another beauty full of intelligence and sensitivity. Stuttering between fast breaths, Clancy told Jack he'd like to be buried at the ranch. His papers were in order, he'd said. He had few possessions. They'd go to Tyler and Lindy, he promised, as if he was a real uncle. "I've always loved you, Jack," he'd said. "You're the best friend I ever had."

The *Arabia* sailed on, and after Clancy and Nafrini had gone, Jack stormed off in pursuit. Clancy said other things. Apologies and memories came rushing out of him. Jack couldn't take them all in. "Save it for later, old boy," he'd said. Was it fair? Jack only knew that Clancy needed fast help if he was to survive. They didn't need a lot of running off at the mouth.

The steamer hadn't gotten far. Jack could see it in the southern distance. He didn't think much. He didn't want to think. There were a couple of things he knew with certainty. The attack against Clancy hadn't been random. The antiquities services officer had been outside with Jack when it happened. That meant whoever was responsible was on the *Arabia*.

With powerful hooves pounding the desert floor, the eager-to-please horse caught the steamer and kept going. After reaching a considerable distance, Jack leapt from the horse, then dove into the Nile, catching the north-flowing current. An aggressive swim to the west, combined with the water's movement, put him on a direct path toward the *Arabia*. Something special carried him onward. Was it divine energy or self-righteous fury that removed fatigue, hunger, and sentimentality? It gave Jack strength, whatever it was, and he strapped himself to it.

Despite this, challenges remained. Plans needed rational thought. He couldn't make any plans. He had no idea what to do with Krüger. He remained beside himself, wild and violent. Swimming and gliding with the current, he saw no passengers on the *Arabia*. He did, however, see the dragoman standing on the main deck, port side. Perhaps the tourists had retired to their cabins and saloons. Moving fast toward the ship, incapable of slowing down, Jack slammed into it. He grabbed a porthole, pulled upward, and then grabbed the lower deck rail. Heaving himself from the river, he threw water from his eyes with a flick of his head. It was then he saw a flash of color, the result of a brutal kick to the face, which plunged him backwards into the Nile. Even before rising for air, he tasted blood. The shock so stunned him that he froze, and it took some time to gather his senses. Surfacing, he saw the dragoman standing at the rail.

While the steamer pushed southward the dragoman kept his eyes on Jack. He walked the length of the *Arabia* as a guard against Jack's ability to climb aboard. Was it he who stabbed Clancy? How could such a theatrical figure surrounded by tourists go unnoticed? Jack swam back to land. He removed the puzzle from his thoughts. He had no patience for mysteries, and no patience for pain. After climbing out of the river and up onto the embankment, Jack staggered to his horse. He mounted, and with a bloody grimace charged again. This was a battle to the death. This was vengeance as much as anything else.

****

Jack's second attempt to board the *Arabia* necessitated a more discreet approach. He swam beneath the water's surface. Above him, the sun blazed, blinding and solid for a moment, and then shimmered erratically owing to the water. When he needed air he gently stabbed at the sky with only his face. He affected no commotion this time, just let the north-flowing river connect him to the steamer. He didn't allow for a look to the lower deck. He couldn't afford the greater risk of being seen. When the time came, and the massive bulk of the *Arabia* nearly smacked into him, he reached up to the porthole. Holding tightly, the ship carried him a ways, and only then did he hazard a glance to the rail. Seeing no one, he swiftly climbed aboard.

With the observation deck above, he ducked beside the windlass. He then moved, crouched beneath windows, outside the dining room wall. Once past a boiler, he crossed to starboard in case an unseen person had initiated pursuit. Hurrying along the starboard rail, he stopped at the halfway point where a long chain of cabins began. He then descended a set of stairs.

Up ahead, passing cabin door after cabin door, with his back facing Jack, was a man in a blue suit and Panama hat. The man pulled a key. Jack brushed dripping hair from his face, and with a soft stride went after him. When the man inserted his key in a cabin door, Jack quickened his pace. The door opened, and Jack rushed him. From behind, he viciously gripped the man's throat with a bicep and forearm. With his free hand Jack shoved down on the back of the head. Having entered the cabin, he then kicked the door shut behind him and slowly brought the man to his knees.

Jack told him he had a knife, and if he made a sound, he'd get it in the back, just like the fellow in the tomb. A few moments later, without much effort, the man was gagged and tied to a chair. Jack changed into one of the man's freshly pressed suits. He picked the Panama hat up from the floor, fallen during the struggle, and was out the door.

Omar Tahan, a figure of importance, would likely be located on the promenade deck, as it afforded a slightly better view. With this in mind, Jack raced to the higher level. He kept the hat low, just above his eyes. Undoubtedly, others on board the *Arabia*, in addition to the dragoman, knew his face. He had to remain inconspicuous.

From behind, a female voice muttered, "Excusez-moi, monsieur."

Jack turned to a woman in a floral print shirt with matching headscarf. "Oh, good," Jack said, interrupting an unspoken question that shaped her bright red lips into a circle. "Perhaps you could help," he quickly continued. "I wish to pass a message to Mr. Tahan. Do you know his cabin? I was told but can't seem to remember."

She had friendly chocolate-brown eyes. "I do not recall seeing you before," she said, with a French accent, adding a high pitch to the last word of her sentence. "Here I thought I had been introduced to each and every passenger."

"Please forgive me for not being more social. I'm Mr. Hunter. American."

"Cabin fourteen. On the lower deck." She brushed past Jack. "J'espère que Monsieur Tahan sait combine il est chanceux," she added without a glance back.

Dismissing the French woman from his thoughts, Jack hurried from the promenade to the lower deck. He passed number six, where his captive remained, and as the numbers climbed higher, he knew he was getting close. He wished he had evidence. All he really had was a story. Would Tahan cancel his speech based on the word of a stranger? The problem took a back seat when, at the hallway's far end, imposing in his theatricality, the dragoman appeared.

Jack froze, then remembered the number six key in his trousers. He retrieved it, unsure whether the dragoman recognized him. No sudden movement came, no expression of surprise, although the dragoman was walking in Jack's direction. With a simple turn, the lock flipped, and Jack opened the door. Inside, he immediately saw he was in a more vulnerable position than he'd thought. Someone had been watching him, aware of him, ahead of his every step. Jack shut and locked the door.

The captive was gone. He was nowhere. He'd obviously been set free as soon as Jack left the cabin. It wasn't possible, and yet, no matter how long Jack looked at the empty chair where the man had been tightly gagged and bound, it remained empty.

Jack whirled to the sound of a click. He saw the doorknob jiggle, and considered that his enemies—who could tell how many there were—knew his whereabouts. He stepped lightly to the door and put an ear to it. The knob turned right and left. Thankfully, the lock continued to prevent any significant movement. Would the dragoman bust in? He easily had the power to do it.

A profound stillness followed. For a while, Jack heard only the small distant sounds of birds outside over the Nile. His heart beat uncontrollably against the peaceful quiet. He was trapped. How could it have come to this? He'd underestimated his adversaries. Would Max ever learn what happened to him? He cursed the arrogance that brought him here.

After several moments Jack convinced himself that whoever was on the other side of the door had left. He inhaled and exhaled deeply, trying to shed the panic that threatened to cripple him. Quietly, he checked the cupboard, wardrobe, and lavatory for anything useful, but came up empty. He considered walking out, taking a shot at making it safely to cabin fourteen, but was being watched. It had to be the case. He'd never make it. Crying out for help would present massive hurdles in his effort to convince Tahan he was the target in a plot involving political assassination. There had to be something Jack could do. He was missing it.

Again, the doorknob jiggled. Along with it came the sound of a male voice saying, "I can't believe I locked the door with my key inside. Sorry for the trouble."

"It is no trouble," replied an Egyptian. "Do not worry."

A key slipped into the lock. Jack rushed to the floor and scrambled under the bed. The door opened. "You've been most helpful," the man said. A third voice said something in Arabic. There followed some back and forth. Jack couldn't understand any of it. A strange clatter might've been a couple of dishes. Looking out from under the bed, Jack saw six feet. Someone left, and the cabin door closed. Two people remained.

"Do you really think hiding will gain you anything more than a few seconds?"

Jack knew the voice. It was a deep voice. His earlier encounter with the man could still be tasted between rattled teeth. Jack revealed himself. He saw the poor occupant of the number six cabin standing, shivering and confused, next to the dragoman. A gun appeared, pressed to the frightened man's ribs. Jack stood. As he did so, the dragoman extended his gun arm, now pointing the German Luger directly at Jack.

CHAPTER NINE

Alone in cabin number six for what seemed hours, Jack and the unfortunate traveler he dragged into this mess, sat gagged and tied to wicker chairs, unable to wiggle free, despite considerable effort. Every heartbeat nudged Jack closer to the edge of panic.

A man entered, alone. Not the dragoman; instead a thin, strange-looking fellow, wearing a Stetson boater, and cream-colored suit. His hair and mustache were dark brown over a wrinkled face. After closing and locking the door, he turned to Jack and removed tinted glasses.

"Your tenacity is commendable," said Mirko Krüger, speaking with the same wheedling menace Jack heard before. The mustache was removed next, and the placid face from the fire-lit caverns returned. Terror flushed through Jack up to his eyeballs, and it must've been visible, because Krüger next said, "Oh, do not worry. I am no longer carrying the knife I used on your friend.

"It is an interesting business we are in, is it not?" he went on. "Like other businesses, it requires time to get to be good. Perhaps the most useful thing that comes with time is the ability to spot others from the same profession." Krüger stepped to the window where the light was waning. As the light hit his hair, the artificial brown coloring became even more noticeable. "The body language, the look in the eye; the thought processes of the individual, begin to read easily. You recognize them because you too know well the same thought processes. You know what such a person is thinking because you have the unique experience of having been there yourself. Seeing you in Imbaba, I thought to myself, this one is different, but not different enough."

Jack wondered why he was being kept alive. Poison was a silent killer, proven with Kalem. However, Krüger didn't expect Jack. Maybe he had no poison. Maybe that's why he seethed when mentioning Jack's tenacity. Was he unprepared for murder beyond taking out Tahan?

"The first American I got was some months back after I recently returned to Cairo. I had been affecting a Russian accent. I was at a party on the rooftop of the Continental Hotel, where waiters carry champagne to white-linen-draped tables. Guests were enjoying the sunset over the domes and minarets of Cairo's older district. I passed a young American. Someone asked him where he was from. St. Charles, Missouri, he said. The American then changed the subject. I thought this peculiar. I thought, he is not really from St. Charles, or he is from St. Charles and running from his past, seeking escape. Also possible is that both are true. What kind of a man lies about his past, runs from his past?

"I followed him. I discovered his whereabouts, had a man send him a package, and explain it is from a female admirer. The package needed a signature, you see. As you are no doubt aware, spies write small. As they work, they write down observations, discoveries on tiny pieces of paper. They cannot very well run around with notebooks. Over time, they develop a history of inserting slivers of miniscule notes between broken seems of jackets and shirts. It is a great way of passing information. You can hand a jacket to someone, and little would anyone guess you are handing over months of fieldwork."

Smiling, Krüger moved away from the window, clasped his hands at his back, set his legs apart, and faced Jack directly, again reviving his military posture. "The American's handwriting turned out to be small. That was the second clue, you see. I then befriended the man. Routinely, we went for coffee. One day I had two men go to the café as strangers. I asked that they argue about the revolution. I waited for the American to comment on it. He did not. Once again, I was pretending to be Russian, so would it not make sense that he would have questions on whether the revolution should occur? A normal American salesman would have curiosity. Would he not ask a Russian, who was clearly alive during the Russian Revolution, something about his thoughts?" Krüger gracefully snatched his cigarettes from a pocket and lit one. "An American businessman is in Cairo to make money, is he not? If a revolution occurs, would it not impact his business? Clearly, he would have said something, unless he was accustomed to keeping things to himself, unless he did not care about the future of commerce in Cairo. If a man carries himself like a spy, writes like a spy, acts like a spy, I am left with little choice but to think he is a spy.

"Almost immediately afterward, more Americans came with the familiar body language, the lonely eyes. It takes experience to shed these things. Ironically, this loneliness is often a result of loyalty. You see, for the greatest of spies there can be no true loyalty. The whole world is an enemy. Trust is the beginning of the end."

Krüger pulled a watch from his pocket and checked the time. The light in the cabin had taken on the soft peach-colored dimness of approaching twilight. His pleased-with-himself smile looked frozen, mannequin-like. He carried on, saying, "In October 1928, I convinced al Husseini, the Mufti of Jerusalem, a man who believed me to be loyal to him and his people, to have the Islamic call to prayer performed next to the Wailing Wall, as the Jews conducted their prayers. The Jews protested these provocations, and already existing tensions increased. When some time later, riots turned into a massacre, I participated, killing not just Jews, but Arabs too. Not knowing, perhaps not caring about the actions of a German at such a time, they continued only to point fingers at one another. I had learned that the more outraged people become, the more easily they can be manipulated. Loyalties only defeat possibilities, you see. Again, the great spies know this.

"A short while later I was in China. Sun Yat-sen died from liver cancer, and Chiang Kai-Shek was leading the Chinese Nationalists. He made the decision to purge the Communists. Consequently, he needed a foreign backer to fill the gap the newly removed Soviets left. He turned to Berlin. We helped the Chinese a great deal, and they trusted us. They trusted us too much, you see. When Hitler saw the Japanese as the obvious superior power he ordered the removal of all German advisors from China." Krüger checked his watch a second time. "Now they have civil war, and an eventual Communist victory seems likely. Such is the way of things," he said, while moving to the door. Before leaving the cabin, he stubbed out his cigarette, and added, "Once again, sir, your daring was a delight to behold. It is a shame to see it end."

Shortly after the man who stabbed Clancy left, Jack worked himself into a sweat, boiling with more rage than he felt throughout this entire wretched day. Trying to free his wrists, he nearly ripped off his skin. Snarling into the gag, he rocked his chair sideways. The other restrained man did nothing. Jack soon fell against him, and remained tilted, suspended on just two chair legs. While the other sat unmoving, Jack tossed and bounced, pressuring the legs with as much turbulence as he could muster.

The legs buckled when a smattering of creaks gave way to a snap, and then another. Jack crashed into a splintered mess. A shot of pain launched upward along his spine. His ferocious jostling had, however, produced the desired effect. With an ankle free, he was able to grip one of the broken legs with one hand, and use its shattered end to pick at the knot binding the other.

In Arabic, a male voice spoke. It was amplified throughout the steamer. Unless another man was introducing the speech, it could only have been Tahan. Either way, Jack had no time. Stabbing and poking at one of the ties that fastened his wrists to the chair gave him none of the speed he so desperately needed. He awkwardly stood. The wicker chair remained hugging his back. With as much force as possible in such a cramped space, he slammed into a wall, but nothing changed. After another failed attempt, he shifted strategies, diving back-first onto the floor. Having now successfully crushed much of the woven wicker into loose threads, he found freedom. Scrambling to his feet, he removed his gag, and then removed the gag on the other man.

"Where did they take you?" Jack demanded to know. "When they pulled you out of here, where did they take you?"

The man was British, a fact revealed when he spoke. "What a bloody outrage! I assure you, you'll receive no kindness from me."

With both hands, Jack gripped him by the ears, and thundered through gritted teeth, "I'm trying to prevent an assassination. Give me the cabin number."

"Cabin thirteen," he hesitantly replied.

Leaving the man, Jack dashed into the hallway. He ran to cabin thirteen, and found the door wide open. It looked unoccupied, mysteriously so. Had the British man made a mistake? A steward passed the window. He looked like a ghost against the dimming twilight. Jack rushed back out into the narrow hallway, flew by the cabins, and rushed up the steps to the port side deck.

Outside, the speech was heard more clearly. Tahan spoke from the bow. His words came interrupted occasionally by generous applause. Meanwhile, Jack caught the steward mid-stride. "I beg your pardon," he said. "The man in cabin thirteen is gone. Someone was there. Cabin thirteen? Do you know where he is?"

"The man was most peculiar."

"Where is he?"

"I helped him into a rowboat. He said it was imperative he leave at once."

"He must still be here," Jack insisted.

"No, no. Come. I show you."

After being led to the stern, Jack's vision was directed a good distance from the *Arabia*. Darkness obscured everything. Nevertheless, a cream-colored suit and Stetson boater were visible. Arms moved as though rowing a boat. Krüger was leaving. There could be no doubt about it. Perhaps he wanted an alibi, Jack thought. That was why he asked the steward for assistance.

A boom cracked the sky wide open. The world brightened with a sudden flash. For the briefest of seconds Jack thought it was gunfire, but then another explosion came, followed by a colorful shower of light. Fireworks thundered and crackled. The steamer and the Nile waters flashed white, red, and green. Applause from the crowd at the front half of the ship intensified. The speech couldn't continue after such a display. It had to be over. Had the assassin been stalling for this moment? Was a sky filled with deafening blasts meant to camouflage the killing shot?

Jack leapt upon the rail, climbed to the upper deck, and swooped over rolled canvas curtains. He landed on the *Arabia*'s roof. With blasts continuing, he ran the length of the steamer from stern to bow, passing the smokestack and water tanks. Below, the crowd was visible. It was a tuxedo and gown affair. A number of men wore tarbooshes, but only one stood before a microphone. Omar Tahan—it had to be him. He smiled and humbly accepted the excited crowd's enthusiastic adulation.

Beside Tahan stood the dragoman. He slipped a hand into his robes. He was going for a gun. Jack knew it. This was the moment. Jack had to stop it, but the rapid-fire flashing and booming in the skies disoriented him. He saw

Clancy bleeding, and Krüger escaping. It was all too much. What was he doing here? he wondered. He then took a fast breath and rattled the infernal fears from his head, and narrowed his thinking to the task at hand. After a couple of steps back, he took a running jump, flying off the observation deck.

A pistol glinted. Jack crashed head-first, toppling the dragoman. He rolled away and looked back. The dragoman remained gripping the pistol Jack saw. Dutifully, the dragoman fired a shot at Tahan. Jack went for a second attack. Another shot rang out as the dragoman swung his gun arm.

Jack expected blood and pain, a bullet ripping through his chest, but felt nothing. The dragoman, on the other hand, collapsed, hitting the hard wood floor of the bow, his colorful robes darkened with blood. The shot to Tahan had missed, while an armed member of his security managed to put a bullet in the dragoman's head.

CHAPTER TEN

The next morning, Jack was in a town called Menouf, a couple of hours north of Cairo. The hospital there admitted Clancy the night before. Enough blood was lost to require a transfusion. The knife entered his abdominal cavity. He required surgery, but thankfully he made it. For several days to come he'd be weakened, but would survive.

Nafrini was with him. She said Clancy had awakened for a while, bursting with fits of nostalgia, talking about his early days as a pilot. She told Jack, "He remembers reading in his father's newspaper about the first flight ever."

"He would've been nine at the time."

"He said, 'In my young mind, I thought that if we could get above the trees, it wouldn't be much further to get to the stars.'"

Nafrini's tenderness comforted Jack. "I've no doubt he appreciates you being here with him," he said. Jack couldn't imagine losing Clancy. His spirit held so much warmth, so much humanity, that even the most jaded of men could regain hope from his presence.

Clancy went on sleeping, and Jack telephoned Deputy Minister Haka Mahmoud, who told him the rioters had dispersed when the sun came up. There'd been fires, businesses damaged, cuts and bruises, but nothing too terribly serious. While still aboard the *Arabia*, Jack had asked Omar Tahan to ring the Deputy Minister and get officers to Ramses Station to search for Mirko Krüger. They got a story in the papers about the assassination. Included was the photograph of Krüger as a younger man. Though not a surprise, it was still a disappointment when Jack was told no one had seen him.

Mahmoud also told Jack he'd called Professor Nazari, and asked if his excavation equipment had been returned. Police business, he'd explained, and was then told the equipment had in fact been returned. Mahmoud demanded the address for whoever took the equipment, and the professor, anxious to avoid scandal, complied. Mahmoud had no time, however, to track down the lead. Being Deputy Minister required him to write an official report on the incident in Beni Hasan, and so he was on his way south.

Nearly three hours later, Jack was in Cairo holding the address on a rumpled slip of paper. He'd stopped and picked up a Browning 9mm from Mahmoud's old Abwehr agent friend. It had Third Reich markings on it. Perhaps not coincidentally, he was in the area where the overnight rioting had occurred. Would he find nothing but a burned out building? It was a commercial district, its affluence clear from some newer buildings with sculpted surfaces done in Egyptian motifs such as lotus flowers and palm leaves. In the end, the address the professor provided led not to a burned out building, but a vacant one.

The space was large, empty, and eerily quiet, seeming to hide every detail of its past life. Inside, Jack ran an index finger along a window sill and found dust. In the pursuit of justice, nothing felt lonelier than a dead end, Jack thought. How far would he go to get the Nazi? he wondered. Despite Krüger's advanced age, he'd remain a danger. Standing in the middle of nothing, Jack asked himself what would've happened had Krüger succeeded? Omar Tahan would be dead. No one would've known of Krüger's involvement. Escaping by train would've been hassle-free.

It hadn't worked out that way though. Jack and Clancy had seen Krüger and survived. The Nazi no longer had anything left to bargain. Things had changed for him, and it made sense he now found himself in a desperate situation. If the gold was meant to support revolution, then the divers likely had been Egyptian, likely members of The Brotherhood, and if The Brotherhood no longer had anything to gain from him, would they provide a hideout?

Self-preservation always necessitated that Krüger keep his most trusted allies to a handful. The one piece of Krüger's plan that remained unchanged was that the dragoman was gone. They had to know going in that an assassination carried out on the bow of a steamer meant fast death, or a straight shot to the slammer. One could suppose, Jack thought, assuming the dragoman lived alone, that his home was now empty. It wouldn't remain so for long. Investigators would get his address and tear the place apart, but it could take a while before they reached that point.

Thomas Cook & Son's moorings were just downstream from a bridge that connected metropolitan Cairo to the Island of Gezira. There were no steamers on the Nile when Jack arrived, just a few small yachts with tall sprouting masts. He stood, staring thoughtfully, as the river reflected blinding sunshine like polished steel.

"May I be of some assistance?" a man asked in English. The question was from a short man smoking a cigar. Sweat stains ringed his hat, and a round torso pressured the buttons of his shirt.

"Are you with Cook?"

Shaking hands, he answered, "Gibbons is the name. Yes."

"Hunter," Jack offered politely.

"Looking to arrange a voyage?"

"I'm an attorney from New York," Jack lied. "You no doubt heard what happened on the *Arabia*? A shame. Forty-five passengers traumatized, and knowingly put in danger. A man was stabbed. Despite an obviously troublesome situation, the *Arabia* carried on, and then there was the unfortunate shooting. Lawsuits will certainly be forthcoming. In all likelihood, passengers will band together, put your company out of business. Oh, don't look so glum. That dragoman was a revolutionary. Cook & Son obviously knew nothing about it. Proof of his subterfuge is what we need. How do we get proof? The best way is to get into his home. Police will get there of course, in due time, but can they be trusted? I don't think so. Many of them are revolutionary sympathizers themselves."

With more than a little desperation, the man asked, "How about I give you the dragoman's address?"

"You expect me to search his home?"

Lines of sweat raced down Gibbon's moon-shaped face, as he said, "I am very sorry. I am not thinking clearly."

"Alright," groaned Jack, "I'll do it, but don't be surprised if I charge more for my services."

"Of course."

Zamalek was a wealthy neighborhood on the northern end of the Island of Gezira. Imported trees and plants had overgrown much of the area. Jack remembered Nafrini saying that the body of Clancy's friend was found at the nearby Sporting Club. Suddenly it wasn't too difficult to figure out who put him there. How had a dragoman come to live among such luxury? It seemed more than a little ironic amidst cries for revolution.

Gibbons mentioned a bungalow with an oak tree out front. Jack asked his driver to park three doors down. As the driver left, Jack placed a hand in a pocket finding comfort in the grip of the Browning 9mm. In the driveway, parked alongside the oak tree, was a 1930s Hudson. Jack saw no one around. The street seemed strangely deserted. It was mid-day, however, and people tended to avoid the heat if they could—especially those well off.

Assuming a casual pose, Jack stepped to the back of the house, no longer looking toward the bungalow with the tree. He hit shaded areas beneath exotic greenery that billowed into the skies. Was Mirko Krüger desperate enough for this? It didn't seem to fit. The Nazi had been a successful secret agent for four decades. He had to have a contingency plan for being sought after once the gold was gone. Jack recalled the feeling he had when they first arrived in Cairo; lost, impatiently stabbing the dark, hoping to find something to hang their hats on before going home.

Crossing properties, he came to the back of the dragoman's bungalow. From behind a standalone garage, he looked to the back windows. He saw no movement, no lights, heard no radio. Crouching, he ran, ducking beneath the largest window as he made his way from the garage. Closer now, he listened again, hearing nothing until a gun-blast startled him. Fragments flew from the wall. Another blast hit the windowsill. Shots were coming from the garage. He pulled the 9mm and fired back, then pivoted, and shot out the window. He leaped through a crashing wave of glass, landing inside the bungalow and scurrying on hands and knees for cover.

Jack's heart pounded as if it wanted to fly from his chest. Leaning against a cabinet, he listened for footsteps, but heard nothing. He waited. Had he entered a trap? How could Krüger have known he was coming? He saw him exit the cab; he had to. Silence was now absolute. Jack struggled for focus. So many things raced through his mind at once.

Jack heard the engine of the Hudson roar to life, and knew the Nazi was getting away. Jack ran to the front door as tires screamed against concrete. Once outside, he saw the Hudson's back swerve onto the road, and recognized Krüger behind the wheel, shifting gears. As the automobile lurched forward, Jack aimed and popped off a shot with the 9mm. He missed and took another shot. A tire blew, but the car kept going.

Jack ran after the vehicle. Krüger looked back, and fired. After dropping and rolling through grass, Jack shot again, this time shattering the Hudson's back window.

Stopping, Krüger got out, rounded the car, and ran into a thicket of trees. With eight rounds remaining, Jack chased the Nazi. He followed into shadows. Moving quickly, he tried keeping his senses fully alert, watching, listening, ready for anything. After a while, having covered much ground, Jack thought he lost him. However, distantly, where the trees became fewer, he spotted the Nazi. Jack was certain it was him as he still wore the same cream-colored suit from the day before.

Jack didn't run. He walked. He took a moment to recall the evil behind the Nazi's actions. Hunting a man in this way rattled his sense of justice. He moved through the forest, unsure, asking himself if he'd ever feel anything other than self-righteous for killing Mirko Krüger.

The forest opened. Gardens, immaculately manicured with the sharp-cut pathways of an English estate, stretched to the island horizon with Cairo in the distance. Structures showcased detailed carvings and patterns typical of Islamic design. A richly ornamented pavilion stood next to a placid lake like something out of an Arabian fantasy. Jack saw Krüger enter the largest structure, the Palace Hotel. He went after him. Seeing guests and groundskeepers, he pocketed the Third Reich pistol.

Through a decorative arcade, Jack entered a world of grandeur. The flooring was chessboard patterned. A sitting room contained a fountain, screens, oriental rugs, palms, and bamboo. Jack crossed to a hall and staircase. Above him, Krüger stood, facing away from Jack. He struggled. Five men held him and rifled his pockets. A gun was pulled. Krüger tried to break free, and the men became rougher with him. He was hauled away while Jack watched from below.

Three men, similarly fashioned, carrying the same seriousness of expression as the men above, approached

Jack. With an Arabic accent, one of the men said, "A friend requests your presence."

Curious, Jack followed. He wondered about the surreptitious manner of the Deputy Minister. Why would he fear being seen? Why the secrecy? Nothing further was said. No questions were asked, as the men escorted Jack to a guest room. When the door opened, Jack was surprised. He'd expected Mahmoud. However, standing before him, alone in the room, was none other than Marshall Kitchener.

"You have done your job. Your country is indebted to you."

Jack said nothing. The presence of Marshall Kitchener in Cairo darkened everything. For several days— ever since the night Mahmoud recited a short Mirko Krüger biography in fact—Jack refused to acknowledge nagging suspicions. The thin old man stood, elegantly attired, smiling in the way a rich man does to a poor man's folly. The room was ornate, stately. Jack recalled it was built to impress Empress Eugenie, and had undoubtedly succeeded.

"You have my gratitude and congratulations," Marshall Kitchener went on. A blue-gray blemish, barely visible above his left eye, was all that remained from crashing into a tree in Texas.

Finding his voice, Jack said, "Tell me about you and Mirko Krüger."

"He is now in our care. You did more than we could have expected. We have information we did not have. As example, we now know el-Fakhoury is supported wholeheartedly by The Brotherhood. This is good information. Omar Tahan will have a chance, thanks to you. All of Egypt will have a chance."

"Clancy's lucky to be alive. A lot of people aren't alive."

"Information is occasionally more valuable than the individual fighting for it. All who enter the profession are aware of this."

"Aqaba? Right? You knew Krüger in Aqaba many years ago."

"You search for clarity."

"Certainty."

"Something I could never provide. No one can."

"I'm guessing you have the gold."

"Gold?"

"Don't be stupid."

"I am merely surprised you think it would mean something to me."

"So you don't have it?"

To that, Marshall Kitchener said nothing.

"What's this about?"

"A great many things, I suspect."

"Such as?"

"You will have to accept a certain amount of secrecy, Mr. Hunter. Comes with the territory, I'm afraid."

"I don't like secrets."

Marshall Kitchener turned in the direction of a chair with elaborate upholstery and a gilded frame. He faced it without really looking at it. His blue eyes danced, and then he looked again to Jack. "Mr. Hunter, have you noticed during times of war how shifting boundaries become everything? A few have the opportunity to change the world as they see fit. Mirko, myself, and others, have been among those fortunate few. We have used our influence and knowledge to map out new worlds in times of vulnerability. A handful of gold is nothing compared to the power of charting history, taking a prosperous territory and changing the hands of control. Mirko, as a German, found himself in a weakened position after the war. We took advantage of it. He knew we would. That is what we do, after all. Out of desperation he decided to see what he could do on his own. He knew that was something we could not allow."

"You sound like him."

"Is that supposed to hurt my feelings?"

"All these men who were killed," Jack said, "you knew these men. Did they know you?"

"Careful, Mr. Hunter."

"They thought they were fighting for something bigger than themselves, but they weren't. You're not representative of any kind of ideology. You're a representative of power. Power for the sake of power. Power because you enjoy it. A lot of good men died."

"Not all of them were good. You'd be surprised. Some were, some weren't. As with most things, the closer you look, the more your vision blurs. I too wish for clarity. How simple life would be if good guys and bad guys were easily revealed." After a pause to punctuate his point, the veteran spy went on. "I wish you the best. You have done well here, Mr. Hunter, as difficult as it may be to see."

When a hand was offered to shake, Jack refused it. Instead, he turned and walked away. "I am not who you think I am," Marshall Kitchener called after him.

Though Marshall Kitchener now had more information, Jack had less. He understood less than before. He wanted finality. He wanted the game to end so he could go home and feel good. After leaving the old man, he walked for hours. A wide corniche gently snaked along the Nile. Banyan trees and lampposts dotted the riverbank. At some point Jack realized he was completely lost, but he didn't care. What he'd seen and heard left him depressed.

The late day sun calmed the city with stretching shadows. He tried to put Marshall Kitchener out of his mind. He wanted to believe Omar Tahan had a chance. He wanted to believe the world was moving in a better direction. Khader, he remembered, told him about the Mahdi's father, Mohammed Ben Ali. The man's followers would prostrate themselves to kiss his footprints, and yet he never unveiled his face to them. When he died, his son inherited one of the fiercest religious confraternities in history. What a strange world, Jack thought, full of strange history.

At the sight of the first star, he thought of Max. He thought back to when they fell in love while stranded in the Amazon, and were saved by Umberto Alejandro Quinto and his staggerwing, and Jack wasn't sure he wanted to be saved. Home at the time meant a return to his first wife. He thought too about when he and Max were at the temple of Xuanzang, on the run from Kyo Mingshu, and Clancy came storming out of the sky in his single-seater P-40. These memories, and scores of similarly treasured moments, brought a fragile smile to Jack's face.

He passed the Egyptian Museum with its relics dating back thousands of years. Unquestionably, there were boats from the tombs of kings who hoped for smooth sailing into the next life. As he thought about it, Jack marveled at the efforts to defy permanent death— mummification, elaborate tombs, the marching of priests and priestesses. He thought he'd strolled near the library he and Clancy visited, and considered going inside, but instead he wandered upon the old Savoy Hotel. Lamplights warmed the late nineteenth century grandeur of it. It was very beautiful. Jack imagined officers and wedding-fixated young women dancing to regimental bands. He imagined a young and dashing Marshall Kitchener among them. Only Jack could see the secrets behind the young man's eyes. Had Marshall Kitchener's whole life been like this, Jack wondered, without a single person he could trust, without one true friend?

Weary from thinking, Jack climbed into a cab and returned to Shepheard's. He drank a gin and tonic in the Long Bar, listened to an Italian named Joe tell stories about serving drinks to famous people, and then moved into the adjoining dining room and downed three beers with a delicious plate of Médaillon de Turbotin Normande. After that he went to his room and slept for eleven hours. When he awakened he called Max and told her they'd soon be home. It felt wonderful to hear her voice.

A few uneventful days later, Clancy was discharged from the hospital. He was told to watch for fluids breathed into his airways, and upon returning to the States, get checked for fluid resuscitation. Clancy stepped into the torrid sunshine, supported by crutches. He told Jack he had time to think, and came to the conclusion he was a lucky man. He'd seen the world, had romances, and survived a number of gutsy adventures. "I appreciate all you've done for me, Jack," he said.

"As a friend, you've always set the perfect example for me, old boy."

"I'm not sure about that, but it's nice to hear."

Jack didn't tell Clancy about Marshall Kitchener. He thought it best that Clancy believe they'd risked everything for a grand ideal, and were heading home triumphant. He made up a story about how the Deputy Minister's men discovered the Nazi hiding in Alexandria, and that he'd no longer be a threat to anyone. Truthfully, Jack had no idea what the future really had in store for him.

A taxi took them to Ramses Station where travelers moved with purposeful strides. The hustle and bustle was urged onward by loud announcements of arrivals and departures spoken in French, English, and Arabic. The Parisian grandeur of the place was infused with elements borrowed from Islamic art. Whistles blared, and among all the crosscurrent foot-traffic, Jack asked about Nafrini.

"She wants to hold onto her traditions," Clancy said. "At the same time, she longs for things to be new. She knows life can't give us everything. It all goes by so fast."

"Indeed it does."

"She said her uncle once told her, 'The greatest thief of all is time.'"

Acknowledgements

Melissa Miller and everyone on the Solstice Publishing team are terrific. I can't thank them enough. My wife, Tracy, has been forever supportive and encouraging. When it comes to her, I marvel at how fortunate I am. Elizabeth Yoo painted the beautiful cover art. My friend, Gilles Verschuere did the design work. To the readers who've read any of my previous books, I recognize you have options—thanks so much for trying something of mine.

About Stephen Jared

Stephen Jared grew up in a small Ohio town in the late 1970s/early 1980s. He was at the cinema every weekend. When considering what he might do as an adult he only had one idea: he wanted to work in movies. In the summer of 1989 he moved to Los Angeles. He was twenty-one years old. Since then, he's appeared as an actor in movies such as *He's Just Not That Into You*, and on television in *iCarly* and *Criminal Minds*. In 2010, he wrote *Jack and the Jungle Lion*, a novel inspired by 1930s Hollywood. Having received much critical praise, Solstice Publishing began releasing his work. *The Elephants of Shanghai* continued on from where *Jack and the Jungle Lion* left off, and went on to take Second Place at the 2013 Hollywood Book Festival. While remaining busy as both author and actor, Stephen is also Associate Producer of an upcoming documentary about movie poster artist Richard Amsel who created classic illustrations for *Flash Gordon* and *Raiders of the Lost Ark*, among others in the late 1970s/early 1980s.

Reviews from the first two Jack Hunter adventures:

Jack and the Jungle Lion

and

The Elephants of Shanghai

"*Jack and the Jungle Lion* may be an affectionate tribute to adventure serials and screwball comedies of the 1930s, but it stands on its own as a great fun read. Featuring an unapologetic coward of a movie star, a beautiful and tough-as-nails animal trainer, a genuinely frightening Peruvian devil, a wise butler, and a fellow who just happens to own a Staggerwing, the story is as entertaining as it is refreshingly free of cynicism. I loved Stephen Jared's first novel, and sincerely hope it's not his last." – AUTHOR RYDER WINDHAM

"... Jared clearly is a lover of classic films, because he gets the setting, characters and breezy atmosphere right. I'm not sure how many people could recreate this era with this much joy and devotion." - CLASSIC FILM BOY

"Again, as he did in *Jack and the Jungle Lion*, Jared delivers a fast-paced, old fashioned adventure yarn peppered with just the perfect blend of hair-raising action and laugh aloud comedic bits to help lighten the tension. Jack and Max are truly likeable characters and it is a treat to see them again as their continued romantic relationship shows no signs of ever getting dull." - PULP FICTION REVIEWS

"*The Elephants of Shanghai* is every bit as entertaining as its predecessor, and then some. Stephen Jared is a fine writer; his prose crackles with witty dialogue, the action remains on full-throttle, and lovers of thrills and spills in fiction will savor every page of this immensely enjoyable book." – ERROL FLYNN BIOGRAPHER THOMAS MCNULTY

"This is your Saturday morning at the flicks, with hair-raising cliff-hanging chapter-ends, humour and lots of pluck. Beautifully written and with a lot of heart. This should make a great TV or film series." – AUTHOR NIK MORTON

www.ingramcontent.com/pod-product-compliance
Lightning Source LLC
Chambersburg PA
CBHW070912030726
47504CB00005B/1564